CELTIC KNOT

BOOK III

MORTAL ENEMIES

Shelley Dorey

DEDICATION

To the wonderful people of Ireland. I look forward to seeing you and your wonderful country again.

To Jim, as always.

And most of all, my sister Corliss, who skated back to me

Contents

One

O wwww!" What the heck was attacking my leg? *Great.* Not only had I landed in a hornet's nest, but it was night and I couldn't see anything. When I tried to jerk away, I couldn't. Something grasped my jeans, scratching through them with tiny, pointy talons. I tried to push it away, but it ripped my finger!

When a low growl rumbled beside me, my hand groped to find Faellin's bulky shape. "Easy, boy. Stay put until I can figure this out." My huge wolfhound growled again, this time ending with a high-pitched whimper. Whatever had ensnared me also had him in its clutches.

Great job, Bernadette! The first time I try transitioning through time and space on my own, and I wind up in some sort of torture chamber! After taking a deep breath to quell my frustration, I froze. What the hell? The scent of flowers now filled my nostrils. *Wait a damn minute...* I angled myself

1

to one side and tried to take a step forward.

A floodlight suddenly switched on, almost blinding me. I squinted and saw a set of French doors and a wide brick patio. A barbeque and patio furniture off to one side were oddly familiar.

"Who's out there? What are you doing in my yard?" A tall guy with white hair stepped outside, holding a baseball bat over his shoulder.

My jaw dropped. *"Dad?"*

The dog let out another growl and started towards the house; I grabbed his collar. "No! Faellin, it's okay."

"Bernadette?" He took a couple steps closer, lowering the bat. "What the devil? Is that you?"

I tried to lunge towards him, but again the needle tug of something painful tore into my pants, preventing any movement. Looking down, I saw my assailant—Mom's rose garden. Shit! I'd landed smack dab in the middle of her prize hybrid tea roses. There'd be hell to pay when she saw that.

"Yeah! It's me, Dad." Now that I could properly see, I pried the pesky thorns from my clothing. I hadn't done so badly for my first attempt at this space/time travel thing. I'd managed to land right in my parents' backyard! Considering that I'd travelled from another dimension, Otherworld, I'd done great!

Dad rushed forward, dropping the bat which bounced onto the brick. Now that I was free of Mom's rosebushes, he scooped me into his arms. The smell of his aftershave and the warmth of his hug brought tears to my eyes. Even though I'd only been gone for a few weeks, it felt like forever since I'd seen him.

He eased away, holding me at arm's length, openly gaping at my clothing. Crap! I was still wearing the rough tunic and pants from Otherworld. And then Dad saw the dog. His eyes practically popped out onto his cheeks.

Saying that Faellin is just a dog is like saying the Empire State Building is just an office tower. What can I say? Faellin is quite literally a dog of war; an Irish wolfhound, only slightly smaller than your average pony. Outwardly placid, but a fierce protector, he is the creature you want at your side if you happened to wander down a dark alley—or if you're being attacked by psychotic gods.

I reached down and rubbed Faellin's ear reassuringly. "I picked up a stray during my travels to Ireland. Faellin's very friendly, don't worry."

Dad kept an eye on the dog as he asked, "Why are you in the backyard, Bernadette? You could have come to the front door like a normal person. You scared me half to death wandering around out here."

"Lanny? What's going on?" Mom stepped out onto the patio. She pushed her glasses farther up on her nose as she bent forward to see who was in her yard. "Bernadette! For Pete's sake, what are—"

"Mom!" I cut off her words as I rushed over to give her a big hug. "I missed you guys so much!"

"She's got a dog, Marion! I can't believe her landlady allows it! And not a little dog either! Did she get a Chihuahua? Or maybe a pug? Nooo! Not my Bernadette! I know they say 'Go big or go home!', but this is ridiculous." He frowned. "I thought your roommate, Darla, was allergic to dogs."

I snorted and took Faellin's collar in hand. "Her name's Darby, Dad. Why can't you ever remember that?"

"Well, maybe if she had a normal—"

"Shush, Lanny." Mom waved him away and zeroed in on me. "Have you eaten? I've got a left-over brisket and some matzah balls. Come in before the house fills with bugs!" As she ushered me inside, the litany continued, "You never call for a month and then you show up in the *backyard* of all places! What on earth were you doing back there?"

She turned, peering at Faellin. "Is he housebroken? I can't have him ruining my Persian rugs, Bernadette. Maybe he should stay outside."

I grabbed her hand and led the way into the family room. "He's fine, Ma! Faellin would never do that. If you've got any dessert left, I'll take that."

My mouth watered at the thought of something sweet. Weird. I had never been much of a dessert person. Maybe this goddess thing was changing me after all, giving me the same sweet tooth Lugh and Angus had.

"Don't give her the chocolate rugelach! I was saving those for tomorrow." Dad laughed as he herded Faellin inside the house.

"Enough, Lanny. She needs to eat! And as far as you're concerned, remember what your doctor told you. You've got to watch your sugar intake." Mom proceeded to lead me to the kitchen.

I smiled as they nattered at each other. It wouldn't matter if I'd been away a year. They'd never change, thank goodness. God, it was great to be home!

As she uncovered the chocolate pastries, Mom continued, "The last time we spoke there were Navy Seals outside of our house. They were there for almost a week and then they disappeared. Tonight you just appear in our yard. Are things okay? You're not in trouble, are you?"

"No! Things are good. I can't really talk about why the Seals were here. But that's all over now, Ma. It had more to do with the friends I met in Ireland. They had some powerful enemies as it turned out."

She stared at me. "So, where are they now, these Irish friends? No more trouble for you, I hope. You disappeared when they were here. Not a word from you to let us know what was going on."

"They went back to Ireland before I had a chance to bring them to meet you. I'm sorry. I guess I was distracted by their problems and of course I had to show them the city." I managed an apologetic expression. It was getting easier to tell the little white lies.

There was no point in telling her about Lugh's enemies from long ago and far, far away (as in another dimension!) who showed up to kill him. Or that they had abducted me. Or about Tully the Banshee, who had rescued me and later died in the battle. As far as my stories about Otherworld went, they would probably get me committed to the loony bin.

Mom set the plate of pastries on the table in front of me and slapped Dad's hand when he tried to sneak one. "So, no new boyfriend there, I guess. Speaking of which... that jerk you dated, Paul, called a few times. I told him you'd skipped town."

My eyebrows rose. Not so far from the truth. I looked down at Faellin, who was hunkered down at my feet. For a fleeting moment I thought of Lugh. Would he even miss me after the argument we had before I left Otherworld? He was probably distracted by his stupid 'council' and wasn't even aware of my absence.

Dad folded his hands together on the table. "Your mother told me you quit your job at the cafe. So, are you planning on going back to school?" Without waiting for an answer, he continued, "There's a good community college course available for paralegals. It's only two years and then you could join me at the office. It's not Harvard Medical School, where your brother is, but it's a decent job."

How could I tell them that school was totally not on my radar? The magical dog at my feet could barf gold coins whenever I needed them. Not to mention my own newfound talents. With just a thought, I could conjure up pretty well anything I'd ever want. Just one of the perks of being a Celestial Goddess. This family who'd adopted me, who had showered me with love, would never be able to conceive what that might be like.

"I'll think about it, Dad. For now, I'm good. I got some savings and I'll think of something." I couldn't help the smirk when I asked, "Speaking of my brother, how is Seth? I haven't seen him since early summer." My brother was the golden child I had always resented when we were growing up; he could do no wrong in my parents' eyes. After all I'd been through recently, it seemed incredible that I'd ever felt that way. Seth had gifts and talents, and he had made the most of them, just as I was only beginning to do. "Really, how's he doing?"

Mom answered with enthusiasm. "He's doing great! Top of his class." She took a seat next to me. "I think he's got a girlfriend. He doesn't visit as much on the weekends. It wouldn't hurt him to bring her around. What are we? *Chopped liver?*"

"I'll call him, Ma. He's probably busy studying. You know, it is a four-hour trip by car each way; you don't get to be top of the class without working at it." Another first for me. I was actually sticking up for my older brother? Things had certainly changed in the way I looked at stuff these days.

I chuckled. "Come on, Ma... who would date my dorky brother, anyway?" Okay. Maybe I could still muster up the old Bernadette.

"That'll be enough, young lady." My mother's eyebrows pulled together as she peered at me. "You still haven't told us why you were out in the backyard instead of coming in the house." Her eyes widened. "If that dog has left any 'presents' out there, I hope you've cleaned it up."

Dad grinned. "I hope you threw them over the fence into the Winstons' yard. That son-of-a-gun's mutt left his load three times in my front yard last week. And guaranteed your dog would leave—"

"Lanny! Enough with the toilet humor. What are ya, ten-years-old, for Pete's sake?" Smiling sweetly, my mother turned to me. "Are you staying the night? You can catch a ride into the city with your father in the morning. And you could show me the photos from your trip."

My mouth fell open. I didn't need to pat my pocket to know that I'd lost my phone somewhere during my travels. Shit! I didn't even have a pic of Lugh or Angus. I'd been too busy being schooled by my sister, Flidais, to even think of my cell phone.

I pulled myself to my feet. "Sorry, I should get back to the city." I tried not to wince as I turned to my dad. "Would you call me an Uber?"

"Why? Where's your phone?" He closed his eyes and sighed. "Never mind, I'll drive you."

I shook my head. "No. Thanks Dad, but I know you like to catch the news before bed."

His eyes narrowed. "You lost your phone."

"Yep," I replied with a toothy grin. "You must be a mind reader!" It was hard to suppress a chuckle. Thanks to my long-lost sister, Flidais, I had learned how to read minds.

"I'll call you a taxi," he said, shaking his head. As I watched him pull his phone from his pocket, I wondered if I'd ever tell them I'd met my biological sister and mother when I was visiting Otherworld. Probably not. It might cause them pain. The last thing I ever wanted to do was hurt the people who'd always been good to me.

They were my family, far more than the biological mother I'd met in Otherworld. That woman—Celestial Goddess, actually — tried to kill me more than once. Far from being a nurturing mother, Aine didn't give a damn about me. The only thing she cared about was her nefarious plans for Otherworld. I was nothing but a tool for that goddess' desires. Aine was dead, and I'd be lying if I said I felt the slightest bit of grief.

Aside from me, the only good that came from Aine was my sister Flidais. We got off to a rocky start at first, but Flidais was... well, she was different. Stunningly beautiful, she was snark personified... unless she was with animals in her forest kingdom. She had a quick temper, combined with fierce love. Adding to that, she was a capable Celestial, who had spent years learning the nature of her powers, whereas my lessons had lasted only a few days. Oh yeah, Flidais is different; and I'd have loved her even if she wasn't my real sister.

My mother stood up and grabbed a Tupperware from the cabinet. As she put a bunch of the freshly baked rugelach into it, she murmured, "I don't see her for weeks and she's off again, back to her friends in the city." She handed me the container and sighed. "Call us when you're home." Turning to my father, she cautioned, "Tell the cab company she's bringing a horse with her! They might refuse to accept taking that beast in their car."

I rolled my eyes. "Mom! He's a dog. His name's Faellin."

Her eagle eye zeroed in at something on my leg and she plucked at my pants. She held it up to examine it, and her eyes narrowed. "A thorn! A rosebush thorn! Did that dog do his business in my flowerbed? He's probably killed my prize Peace roses!"

Dad scoffed at her. "What are you talking about? They finished blooming weeks ago!"

I pictured the most beautiful of all roses and when I raised my hand, there it was: a creamy yellow flower tinged with pink around the edges. "Not all of them, Dad. In fact, Faellin sniffed one last rose back there."

She smiled and held it to her nose. "The last rose of the season. Isn't it wonderful? Thank you, Bernadette. I would have missed this beauty if you hadn't found it."

I shrugged. "That's me—taking time to smell the flowers."

My mom was a natural detective, never missing a trick when I lived there, but she hadn't caught the fact that I hadn't walked into the house with it, or that it had just appeared in my hand. Maybe Mom had changed a bit, too.

Whatever. It was good to be home.

Two

The cab dropped me off half an hour later at the two-family building where I shared the upstairs apartment with two of my friends. After ordering Faellin to sit at the building's entrance, I punched in the number code and waited for the buzz that it was unlocked—but nothing happened. I tried again with the same result.

Shit! Nosy Natalie, the landlady, must have changed the code. To make matters worse, I didn't have my phone to call either of my roomies. I buzzed the doorbell, praying that one of them was in the apartment. A few moments later, my roommate Prudence opened the door in person.

Her face knotted with concern when she greeted me. "Bernadette! What the hell happened to you? I was going to call your parents tomorrow, if I hadn't seen you by then." She looked down at Faellin and her jaw dropped. "What's that? You got a dog! And never even ran it by us first?"

She jerked away when Faellin stood to sniff her pajama pants.

I rubbed Faellin's head and urged him into the doorway. "Shh! I don't want Natalie to know. Not yet." It would be fun, though, to see that nosy bitch's face when she found out I now had a gigantic dog. Even better would be her reaction when we gave her notice that we were moving out. But that could wait awhile.

Prudence stroked Faellin's head gingerly. "He's a beautiful animal, but what about Darby? You know she's allergic. I don't think this is gonna work out."

I swept by her. "Sure it will. We'll just load Darby up with antihistamines. Besides, she's already met Faellin."

Prudence ignored me and continued prattling as we walked up the stairs. "You never even answered my texts. I was worried—even though Darby said you were probably hanging out with your new friends."

"I'm sorry, Pru. I *was* with them, but I lost my phone somewhere along the way."

Behind me, she muttered, "There are *stores*, Bernadette. You could have replaced it. By the way, the rent's due tomorrow. Good thing you showed up. Where are your friends now?"

There were no stores, let alone cell phones, where I'd recently been, but now was not the time to get into that. The door to our apartment opened before we reached it, and Darby stood there. She smiled, until she looked past me. "You brought the *dog*? Where's Angus?"

I gave her a quick hug and pushed by her. "Nice to see you too, Darb! Angus and Lugh went back to Ireland. But at least I've got Faellin to keep me company."

"I'd rather have Angus than that dog." Darby muttered before she sneezed, once, twice and a third time. "Where are my allergy meds?" She hurried to the bathroom.

Prudence continued scratching behind Faellin's ears. "See? The dog's sweet, but what about Darby? She can't live in a tiny apartment with this beast." She bent down and made mushy faces. "Such a good boy!"

I snapped my fingers and Faellin came over. "Want some water, fella?" As I grabbed a big mixing bowl to fill it, I continued. "It'll work out, Pru, trust me."

All the lines that I'd rehearsed on the drive into the city vanished. I decided to ease into the situation. "How would you like to live in Manhattan? Even quit your job and take up your artwork full time?"

Darby held a tissue to her nose as she walked back into the living room, giving Faellin a wide berth. "What planet are you *living on*, Bernadette? We're lucky to afford *this* place!"

I set the bowl down and watched Faellin lap it up, sloshing water onto the hardwood floor. Darby had almost been right about being on a different planet.

I smiled and flopped down on the sofa next to her. "Uh... I've kind of... well... " I finally just blurted out the news. "I'm rich now. We can afford to live anywhere we'd like. That's why having Faellin around won't be a problem. Hell! He can have his own room if that helps."

Prudence walked over to me and placed her hand on my forehead. "No sign of fever, but you clearly aren't well, Bernadette." She took a seat in her favorite chair. "How 'bout you share your drugs with us? You're obviously high on something. No, wait. I don't do drugs, but I could probably use a drink. Or twelve."

My other roommate leaned forward and skewered me with a look. "Have you come into an inheritance?" Her eyes widened. "I'm sorry, I didn't mean that. Your parents are okay, right?"

I clapped her knee and grinned. "They're fine! I just left their place. But you're sort of right about the inheritance." It was kind of fun playing this game of cat and mouse with my friends. Fun, that is, until I had to level with them. Who knew what they'd do then?

Prudence's eyebrows pulled together, "An aunt or uncle? Some rich grandparent?" She brushed the trail of slobber from her thigh from Faellin nuzzling her.

"No deaths. But as you know, I've always been curious about my biological parents."

Darby jabbed me in the ribs, knocking me against the arm of the sofa. "Get out! You found them? Did you meet your mother and father? Spill it!"

I sighed, thinking of Aine. Yes, she was my birth mother, but she had been anything but motherly. "Not my father, but I met my mother and sister while I was in Ireland."

This time it was Prudence who jerked forward with wide eyes. "They're *rich*? They're giving you money?" Her head tilted to the side. "How rich? How much money are we talking about?"

I winced, and my voice was soft as I answered, "Warren Buffet rich? Jeff Bezos rich? I don't know... maybe even more?"

Darby and Prudence could have caught flies in their gaping mouths as they stared at each other in silence. Finally, Darby swallowed hard and turned to me. "You're serious. For real? Come. On."

"Yes. I'm totally serious!" I jumped to my feet and raced to the fridge. Hopefully, there was something in there to begin a toast. I grabbed a half empty bottle of wine and some plastic tumblers.

Setting them down on the coffee table, I poured generous portions into each cup. "We've been friends since grade school. It's only right that I share my wealth with you guys! We're going to live in a *penthouse*, girls! No more menial jobs or fighting rush hour in the subway. We're taking limousines, baby! *Cadillac* limos! Wait! No! *Rolls Royce* limos!

Each of them grabbed a wine glass and raised it high, bumping their glasses against mine. "To Bernadette's mother and sister! To Bernadette!"

I held up a hand, signaling for them to stop. "Not to my

mother. But definitely to Flidais!"

Prudence's eyebrows rose. "Flidais? Is that Irish? Weird name. But why not toast your mother?"

I sank down next to Darby again. "She's not the nicest creature you'd ever have the misfortune to meet, but Flidais's cool. You'd like her! You'll meet her someday. She and Angus—"

"What?" Darby turned so quickly that she slopped wine onto her knee. "What about her and Angus?"

The breath left my body as I looked at her wide eyes. I sighed. Why'd I have to bring that up? I'd had no idea that she'd actually fallen for Angus after that one crazy afternoon they'd spent together getting their freak on. But it stood to reason. He was totally hawt and charming, not to mention an Irish Fae Prince. Of course, she'd fall for him... bad.

I reached over and squeezed her shoulder. "It was love at first sight, I'm afraid. Angus is absolutely crazy about her."

It was Prudence's turn to sigh. Again, her face twisted as she spoke. "Hang on! Let me get this straight. Your friends were here in New York. Then you said that your mother and sister were in Ireland. And now you say this Angus dude hooked up with your sister. Was she here, or did you go back to Ireland?"

Shit. Prudence had always been the brainy one. I took a deep breath and weighed my words. "She's in Ireland. We went back there for a while and they fell in love."

Darby jumped in, an edge to her voice. "Humph! So he fell for her. No offense Bernadette, but I think your sister must be a slut. How else would she get him to fall for her like that?" Darby's eyes narrowed as she looked at me over the rim of her plastic glass.

I stiffened, and the words leapt from me, "You're one to talk! You knew him all of two seconds before dragging him into your bedroom! Flidais isn't like that. She's really kind of shy, not a slut in the least."

13

Prudence held up her hand like a traffic cop. "No slut-shaming in this apartment, ladies!" Her mouth pulled to the side, sneering when she looked at Darby. "*Two seconds?* That's a record, even for you."

Darby sniffed. "Who's slut-shaming now, Miss Date-for-three-months-before-even-kissing!" She turned to me. "Sorry, Bernadette, but I think I hate your sister."

I slumped for a moment before trying to smile at her. "With the money you'll enjoy, you'll soon forget about Angus." Well, I hoped so, anyway. "Let's have a toast! To our new lives!"

I didn't realize at that moment that all the changes we would experience wouldn't be all warm and fuzzy. No, they would be dangerous. Incredibly dangerous.

Three

After finishing the half bottle of wine, Darby brought out two more she had squirreled away in her bedroom. We kept celebrating through the night and my guard finally slipped. We had exhausted our elaborate plans—the trips we would take, the high points of fashion design for Darby and art school for Prudence—when Darby slurred a question.

"So, do you have this money right now, Bernadette? Can we order up steak and lobster for delivery? Where *is* all of this money?"

I giggled as I pointed at Faellin. "It's right there, guys. My dog's a magic dog!" I held up my fingers, fluttering them in front of my face. "These hands... these are magic, too!"

"Get outta here!" Darby nudged me with her shoulder before bursting into laughter, fluttering her own fingers next to mine. "Me, too! I can type ninety words a minute with no errors."

Prudence scoffed at us. "Okay, enough of the fun and games. Seriously, Bernadette, is your money in stocks? Gold bars or T-bills? I don't wanna hear about no magic dog or magic hands!" She bent to scratch Faellin's head. "No offense, big fella! Such a sweet puppy!"

I stood up and weaved a bit before steadying myself on the arm of the sofa. "I AM serious!" Looking at Faellin's big brown eyes, I snapped my fingers, fumbling a bit until I got it right. "Here, boy! Let's show 'em what you can do."

Faellin hesitated and let out a small whimper before getting to his feet and lumbering over to me. I bent over and rubbed his tummy, as I'd seen Lugh do. It took a little longer than I expected, but then, I'd never done it before. Not to mention I was a little sloshed from all the wine.

"What the hell are you doing to him, Bernadette?"

I held a finger to my lips, shushing Prudence, and continued with the belly-rubbing. And then it began. Faellin started to retch, his ribs contracting with each heave. His mouth opened wide, and with a final gurgle, he spat up a few coins onto the floor in front of him. But he wasn't done yet. Not. By. A. Long. Shot.

He gagged again and a flood of slimy, gold coins burst from his mouth, landing in a wet heap on the floor. I hugged him, holding on for dear life as the floor under me swayed. Oh, boy, was I wasted.

Darby scooted across the sofa and stared at the heap of gold. "Wow!" Now that she was closer to Faellin, she let out an apocalyptic sneeze.

Prudence was in a state of shock. There was no sign of the four glasses of wine she'd just consumed. "I freaking don't believe what I just saw! Pinch me! Tell me I'm dreaming."

I stood up and brushed my hands together in a satisfied manner, smirking at them. "It's real, all right. And that's only what *Faellin* does." Again, I fluttered my fingers.

MORTAL ENEMIES (Celtic Knot #3)

"Get a load of this…" My eyes closed and I pictured the only thing I could think of: Mom's Peace Rose. I snorted, held out my hands and presto! When I opened my eyes, there were daisies in my hands. *Daisies?* I stared quizzically at them.

Lesson number whatever. *Do not conjure items when you're drunk.* I burst into giggles, imagining my sister's voice lecturing me. She'd probably turn me into a wombat for showing off while I'd been drinking.

"Holy cow!" Darby fell back onto the sofa and laughed. "You actually did that! I thought you were full of crap!" She straightened, stood, and almost lurched off the sofa. "Teach me how to do that! I wanna do that magic trick!"

Prudence had sobered up completely at the sight of my conjuring. She stood up and stared at me. "What's happened to you, Bernadette? This isn't some cheap magic trick, is it? You and that dog just made gold coins and flowers appear out of nowhere."

A loud knock on the door covered my awkward hesitation. "Oh no! Nosy Natalie!" Prudence turned to me. "You'd better let me handle this."

But I pushed by her, ignoring her shouts to stop and think for a moment. "I've got this! Maybe I'll turn her into a toad!" But that wasn't quite right, was it? I was a Celestial; not a witch, for Pete's sake!

I opened the door, holding onto the doorknob to steady myself. My lips pursed together before I spat out, "What do *you* want?"

Natalie's eyes opened wider and dominated her little rat-like face. "WHAT? That's all ya got to say for yourself! You're making too much noise, *that's what!*" Her little ratty nose twitched, sniffing the air. "Is someone sick? I can smell vomit even over the alcohol wafting out of your pores! This is the last straw, Bernadette! I thought I'd seen the last of you when you were here with those thugs a few weeks ago. I *prayed* it was the last of you!"

Prudence stepped close to me, nudging me back. "We pay our rent, Natalie. We're entitled to have a celebration now that Bernadette's back in town! And we weren't making a lot of noise!"

I elbowed Pru away. "We're giving our notice, Nosy Parker! This is our last night in your house. We're moving out tomorrow! So there!" I managed to fold my arms across my chest after missing a few times and swayed towards her.

She puffed out her cheeks in disgust. "Good! It saves me from booting you out! And you will still need to pay next month's rent as you didn't give me one month's notice!"

"I got this!" Darby yelled. She and Faellin walked towards us. She grabbed Natalie's hand and thrust a handful of slimy coins into it. "That ought to cover it." Darby smiled at Prudence and me before a new series of sneezes gripped her.

"What the —"

I slammed the door in Natalie's face. The three of us had a group hug before falling drunkenly to the floor. Faellin collapsed with us and wriggled with joy. He let out an excited 'Yap!' and licked my chin.

Eew. Natalie had been right about the puke smell.

Four

The next morning, it was really late when I hauled my butt out of bed. Late even by my standards. I dressed and slowly trudged out to the living room; Prudence and Darby were lounging on the sofa. Darby held an ice pack, covered in a tea towel, to her forehead.

Prudence, cupping a mug of coffee with both hands, tilted her head towards the pile of coins on the coffee table. "There are seventy-five coins there, Bernadette." She glanced down at the tablet propped up on her lap. "By my calculations and double-checking with Google, that's almost twenty thousand dollars."

I wandered over to the kitchen to pour a cup of coffee. "Sounds about right." That was the amount Faellin had barfed up when Lugh and Angus had been in New York. Had it only been a few weeks ago? Crap! So much had changed in such a brief time.

As I sat in the easy chair, Faellin lifted his head and sniffed my leg. I gave his head a rub. "Let me have this mug of Joe and I'll take you outside. I promise." Sinking down in my chair, my hand went to my head, which throbbed painfully. Ugh. Why did I have to drink so much last night?

Darby murmured as she lifted her feet onto the coffee table. "Is that enough to buy a Penthouse? I'm pretty sure it isn't. Maybe I shouldn't have given the money to Natalie last night."

Prudence snorted, "I doubt that would make up the difference, Darb. Seriously, Bernadette, can we move anywhere with that kind of money? Penthouses cost like a *zillion* dollars. I probably shouldn't have quit my job."

I gulped down too much hot coffee and choked. "*You quit?* Already? That was fast." My conservative, cautious friend was full of surprises, but it wasn't a problem. I hoped.

Prudence continued, "It's not too late to suck up to Natalie. Maybe if I ask, she'll reconsider. She did always like *me* best."

I set my mug down with a resounding thud. "No! There's plenty more where that came from, and I'm not talking about squeezing Faellin dry. I can conjure up buckets of cash. Trust me."

Darby's hand fell from her forehead, and she stared at me. "Did you just say *'conjure'*? What are you? Some kind of witch or wizard? I must have heard wrong." She shook her head and slumped lower in her seat.

Now wasn't the best time to keep secrets, not with the way my two besties were looking at me. "Yeah, I said 'conjure'. Like the flowers last night. Look. If I tell you the truth, you must promise me... I mean, a total pinky swear, ladies, you won't tell anyone what I'm about to tell you."

That got their attention. They both shifted on the sofa, leaning towards me, wide-eyed. "I promise." They spoke almost in unison. Good.

I held out my pinky finger for good measure, waiting for each of them to hook theirs into mine. Now that I had the reassurance of the most sacred promise of secrecy, I continued, "I'm a Celestial Goddess. My mother was one and so is my sister, Flidais."

Prudence ran her hands through her short, wavy hair. "A Celestial *goddess*? Honestly Bernadette! If you'd said a witch or a magician, even a sorcerer, I'd have an easier time believing you! But a goddess? C'mon!"

I could see that Prudence was in a state of shock. I closed my eyes and pictured an emerald necklace. Heck, I'm Irish. What other color would I use?

Prudence squealed, "Oh, my God!"

I opened my eyes and laced through my fingers was a necklace of bright silver, inset with glittering emeralds. It was even prettier than what I'd imagined! Prudence grabbed Darby's arm and shook it in astonishment.

"Did you see that, Darb? She did it! Just. Like. that." She snapped her fingers. "You are amazing! But what's this Celestial thing? A goddess is a goddess, right?" She clapped her forehead with her hand. "What am I saying? A goddess? Do we need to bow down to you or something?"

Darby flashed me a look and slipped from the sofa, going to her knees. Immediately Faellin was on his feet, nuzzling her cheek with big slobbery dog kisses. She pushed him away as a sneeze erupted.

"Stop that! Get up! Yes, I'm a goddess." Turning to Pru, I added, "A Celestial is the highest order of god-hood. Lugh and Angus are regular gods, but a Celestial being has even more power."

Darby did a double-take. "*Angus* is a god? Shit! I knew he was special, but a veritable god? No wonder I fell so hard for him!"

My face tightened, and I glared at her. "Hey! I still outrank him! Back on your knees, Darby!" When she had dropped again to the ground, I grinned. "Psych!"

She looked up at me and scowled.

Holding my chin high, and looking down my nose, I assumed a regal tone. "You may rise."

Prudence shook her head. "How does this even *happen*? One minute you're just Bernadette, a waitress hustling for tips. The next you come back from a trip to Ireland and you're a goddess?" The corners of her mouth turned down. "And it happened in Ireland. Not even Greece or Rome."

For the next twenty minutes, I went through the complete trip to Ireland: awakening Lugh from his slumber at the Moon Pond, our battle with Lugh's enemies and my time in Otherworld. When I finished, I reiterated the need to keep this between the three of us. Not even my parents should know. I'd look after them in my own fashion - without the need to jack up their heart medication.

I stood up and smiled. "There you have it. I have to take Faellin outside, now. The poor guy must be bustin' a gut."

It wouldn't hurt to give my friends some time to sit and process all that I'd told them. It was a lot to take in.

***

It was mid-afternoon when the three of us entered the *Gold Exchange* in mid-town Manhattan. I hefted the knapsack full of Faellin's coins as well as ones I'd conjured up and plopped it on Levi's desk as soon as his last customer had walked away.

His eyes widened, and he smiled. "*You again*! What treasures have you brought today?" He glanced at Darby and Pru before recognizing Faellin at my feet. "You have the service dog! What happened to your visually impaired friend?"

"He went back to his own country. I got stuck with the dog, but he's grown on me." I reached down and patted Faellin's head. "He's no problem."

"May I?" Levi's fingers twitched as he held the zipper tab on the knapsack. If a naked woman came running through the exchange, I doubt she would have diverted his attention from the bag.

"Help yourself, Levi. I need to step out while you do your thing. I lost my cell phone and have to replace it." I took a blank check from my purse and handed it to him. "You can deposit my funds into this account, but I'll be back to sign for it in about thirty minutes."

He took the check and glanced at it. "Bernadette! Are you sure? This is an awful lot of coins, judging by the weight."

I shrugged. "I trust you. You treated me well the last time." I signaled to Darby and Pru and then we left, Faellin in step with me.

Prudence gaped at me as we walked up the street. "You're sure about him? That's a lot of coin, as he said himself."

"There's plenty more where that came from, but we don't need to tell *him* that."

As I spoke, it occurred to me that I needed to spread the coins around other dealers too, if I was going to keep doing this. I didn't want to be accused of money laundering or some other crime. Seeing the sign for an electronics store on the next block, I pointed to it. "There. I feel naked without my phone."

Darby frowned. "Why do you need to buy one? Can't you just, you know, do that trick with your fingers and presto... there it is?"

I paused for a moment. "I never thought about that... Yeah. I probably could, now that you mention it. This Celestial thing takes some getting used to. But now that we're this close to a store, I'll just buy one. No big deal."

"Yeah, I think buying one's better. If you conjured up your phone, wouldn't you have to conjure up your own Celestial cell network too? I mean, your phone has to work with a carrier, right? How would that even work?"

"Y'know, I think you're right. I'm definitely buying a

new one."

Darby nodded. "That sounds logical."

When the light turned green, we crossed the street, and I steered Faellin through the crowded crossing. I felt a tug on my jacket, and I jerked around, ready to shout at the pickpocket. My eyes opened wide when I realized who it was, and I had to grab Faellin with two hands to keep the snarling beast back.

"Hello, Bernadette. Long time, no see." My old boyfriend, Paul, smiled at me.

Five

I'll admit it—I was so tempted to let Faellin tear into that jerk. Instead, I glared at him. "Not long enough, Paul. If I never saw you again, it would be too soon."

He held his hands up, smiling sweetly. "Is that any way to treat an old friend? Not to mention a *boyfriend?* Where are the two whack jobs you took up with in Ireland?" He looked at Pru and Darby. "I see you've gone back to Dumb and Dumber."

Darby crossed her arms and huffed. "Screw you, Paul."

"Yeah. In your dreams, skank." His gaze refocused on me. "Seriously, Bern. Things were good between us once. Why don't we grab a drink, or even a coffee, sometime this week? I'd like that, y'know."

"Well, I wouldn't! Especially not after what you did. You helped Lugh's enemy with information on where to find us. And that was after you tried to beat me up in Ireland!"

"What? You *hit* Bernadette?" Prudence took a step closer to Paul, looking down at him. Not only was Prudence an accomplished visual artist, she was a mixed martial pro, too.

25

Darb and I sometimes referred to her as the Amazon Warrior. That, combined with her almost six-foot height, made her an imposing figure.

Paul took a step back. If Faellin's snarls weren't enough to discourage him, Prudence's angry presence certainly was. He shook his head. "Look, I made a mistake! Besides, she tried to ditch me."

"Correction! I *broke up* with you, jerk. That still stands."

Turning to Darby and Pru, I huffed, "Let's go. We're wasting time talking to this loser."

As we continued up the sidewalk, Paul's yells drifted behind us like a rotten smell. "I ain't givin' up, Bern. We had something special between us."

Darby sniffed. "I never knew what you ever saw in that jerk. Now Lugh... That's a guy who would be a good match. And like you, he's a god. Totally hot and—"

"Nope. Lugh has his life, and I've got mine. Not going to happen, Darb." I smiled to take the sting away and held the door for my friends as we entered the electronics store.

My heart ached for Lugh, despite my apparent nonchalance. And it wasn't simply my break-up with Lugh that bothered me; it had gone horribly wrong with Angus and Flidais as well. I had hurt both of them in my clumsy attempt at match-making.

I shook my head. There was nothing I could about it now. Time to focus on the present.

Twenty minutes later, with the newest model iPhone in hand, we were back at the gold exchange. Levi and his brother looked up as we walked to the front desk. "Good timing. I have the paperwork for you to sign." He pushed it across the desk, along with a pen. "You made out like a bandit when your grandmother left you her house. Do you know if there is any more where that came from?"

I nudged Prudence when she shot me a puzzled look. She knew my grandmother was still alive. Her supposed 'death' had been the cover story I'd used when Lugh,

Angus, and I had exchanged the first batch of coins. I'd fill Pru and Darby in later.

Smiling at Levi, I picked up the pen and signed the paper. I blinked when I saw the amount I was signing for. Gold must have increased in value. They would deposit almost thirty thousand dollars in my account.

"Thanks, Levi! It will depend on what I find when we renovate the basement. I might be back!" I tapped the papers with my knuckle and slid them across the desk.

"I certainly hope so. That must be some place you inherited!" Levi signed the papers and gave me a copy.

I turned to leave, but Prudence put her hand on my arm. "Ah... Mr. Meir, you wouldn't happen to know of any good rental agents for an apartment in Manhattan, would you? I'm looking for a new apartment, but honestly, I'm not sure who I can trust."

Levi blinked. "I may be able to help. My nephew Saul works for a firm that handles rentals. Their clients are mostly wealthy Asians who've invested in property here." A quick glance at Prudence and Darby, along with the fact he'd just cut a check for almost thirty thousand dollars, must have reassured him. He pulled out his cell phone and smiled. "The kid owes me a few favors. He'll do right by you. Let me call him."

When Levi spoke with his nephew, I turned, whispering to Prudence and Darby. "Good thinking, Pru. This beats searching on-line and going through all the credit B.S. And a rental is probably wise. It gives me more time to build up a solid base of cash."

Darby mused, "I like the idea of living in Soho. It's right in the heart of everything! Nightlife, restaurants, shopping! This will be so awesome!"

Prudence shook her head. "Soho's too noisy! Now the *Battery* has some real appeal. There's that great park, the view of the water and—"

"How 'bout we flip a coin?" I interrupted them. Both

locations had their merits. I honestly didn't know which one I preferred. I fished a coin from my purse and Darby called it.

Soho it was.

Levi discreetly cleared his throat. When he had our full attention, he grinned. "You're in luck. Saul just finished with a client and was on his way back to the office. He'll be here in ten minutes to pick you up."

Prudence extended her hand to shake Levi's. "Perfect! Thanks for your help, Mr. Meir."

Levi's eyes narrowed. "What is it you do that you can afford Manhattan, if you don't mind me asking?"

Darby hurried to answer. She chirped, "She's a trust-fund kid. We both are!"

I groaned inwardly. *My* trust fund kids.

Faellin let out a little whine, and I reached down to pat his head. "You need to go outside, buddy? C'mon, girls. We should let Levi get back to work." I fluttered my fingers in a wave at Levi before I went out the door; Darby and Pru were right on my heels.

Prudence nudged me as Faellin cocked his leg to do his business on a fire hydrant. "How're we going to recognize this Saul guy when he gets here? How will he know us?"

I rolled my eyes at her. "Trust me, Levi is probably back on the phone with him, giving us a glowing reference, along with our descriptions. Saul probably knows the name of the perfume you're wearing."

A black SUV pulled up to the curb and the window slid down. The glistening white of Saul's smile was the first thing I noticed when he leaned over and called out the passenger window. "Bernadette?"

I walked over and peeked in the window. "That's me! Although, it's my friend Prudence who's looking for an apartment." Feeling Faellin's slobbery mouth nuzzling my hand, I added. "You're good with the dog?"

Saul got out and straightened his tie as he rounded the

front of the vehicle. "Absolutely." Extending his hand to each of us in turn, we introduced ourselves. "C'mon big fella. Let's see if you'll fit in the back." He opened the back hatch and Faellin hopped in.

When we were settled, with me and Darby in the back seat and Prudence riding shotgun, Saul pulled out onto the street. "So, Prudence...where are you living right now?"

She smirked. "In the Bronx. But Darby and I want to be downtown, in the Soho district. We'd like a three bedroom that's also pet friendly, for Bernadette when she visits. We've been at the same apartment for about a year. We've got excellent references."

Saul nodded in approval. "Good. I'll need to check that, and we need a security deposit in advance." He looked her over, appraising the value of Pru's jeans and lambskin jacket. "Three-bedroom apartments in that area go for about five thousand a month."

I leaned forward in my seat. "That's no problem. I can provide the rent for three months today. The balance for the year will be available in a week, provided that we find someplace suitable. And for Pru, being in the Bronx is totally not suitable for her art studies. I'd like to find a place for her immediately, as in today."

His big brown eyes became even bigger as he glanced in the rearview mirror. "Immediately? That's a tall order, Bernadette."

I lightly tapped his shoulder and sat back in the seat, humming the tune that won me the trip to Ireland, via a YouTube contest. The song had worked wonders on gods and mortals alike, and from the looks of things, Saul needed more than a little convincing. Darby looked at me and I watched the furrow between her brows melt away as she, too, listened to the music. Yeah, that song still had a lot of power.

Saul looked in the rearview mirror again, but now there was a mellow look on his face, accompanied by a soft smile.

"I didn't say it was impossible, though. There's a place on Thompson that came on the market this morning. It might do the trick, but I'm hesitant to show it. The cleaners and painting crew haven't had a chance to go through it yet."

Prudence spoke firmly. "We'd like to see it. If it has some potential, we can live with painters coming and going for a while."

Darby concurred. "Absolutely. We just need to get out of that… place, the one we're in now."

I was glad she hadn't slipped and said the word 'dump'. "And they'll be okay with my dog?"

Saul nodded. "As long as he doesn't bark all day or destroy the place. There's a superintendent on site. Charlie's a pretty good guy but he won't allow excessive noise. None of you are partiers, are you?"

I shushed Darby with a hand on her arm and answered quickly, "As I said before, Pru's an art student and Darby's a writer. They won't be any trouble and neither will my dog, Faellin."

Saul looked over my shoulder to where Faellin was watching our conversation. "That's a pretty unique name for a mutt. I guess you weren't expecting much from him when you named him. 'Failing'? He looks more like a 'Barney' to me." He pulled up to the curb in front of a six-storey brick building.

Darby's nostrils flared. "Excuuuuuse me! That dog is a purebred Irish wolfhound! And his name is not 'Failing', it is Faell*in*!" She shot daggers at Saul with her eyes.

Saul held his hands up in mock surrender. "Hey, okay! My bad!"

I couldn't help but grin as Darby sneezed again, with perfect timing. I passed her another Kleenex and chuckled. Yeah, Faellin definitely had grown on her, allergies and all.

The building's exterior was nothing to write home about; plain brick above a street-level restaurant. The main entrance was wedged in between the restaurant and an optician's shop. I saw my disappointment mirrored in Darby's face. So much for the luxury penthouse in Manhattan. Despite the fantastic location, it looked only marginally better than the place we'd left in the Bronx.

Saul must have sensed our reluctance when he turned to Darby and Pru. "The kitchen has been renovated with stainless steel appliances and granite countertops. Have a look before you toss the idea in the trash. It's good value, especially in this area!"

We all got out of the car and I grabbed Faellin's collar when he hopped out. For a moment, the dog stood stock still, sniffing the air. A low growl rumbled in his throat.

"What's with Faellin, Bern? Sounds like he's a bit underwhelmed, too." Prudence scratched behind Faellin's ear. "It's okay, boy. Worst case scenario, we go back to the Bronx. We're paid up for another few days, so technically she can't keep us out."

I shook my head. "No, we'll stay at a hotel before I give Nosy Natalie the satisfaction of crawling back there with our tails between our legs." I patted Faellin's head. "No offense, buddy." Faellin only glanced up at me, before staring down the street again. The ridge of fur along his spine spiked straight up.

I followed his gaze, but there was nothing other than a few teenagers and some shoppers walking by.

Darby asked, "Do you see that sign down there? There's a craft brewery. How handy is that?" She looked down at Faellin. "Maybe he doesn't like the smell of hops."

"Ladies?" Saul interrupted us and held the door. It had all the charm of an old Victorian building, with high wainscoting and hardwood floors. We crowded into the modern elevator.

Saul rocked back and forth on his heels as he watched the numbers on the panel change. "You'll be on the fifth floor. The apartment overlooks the building next door. It may not have the best view, but it's much quieter than a street-side apartment."

When we stepped out, I looked down the hall. There were three other apartments on this floor. The hallway was well-kept, with a clean wool runner over the dark hardwood flooring. Saul opened a final door and, with an extended arm, invited us in.

My friends began to explore while I stopped and openly gaped. I was again reminded to never judge a book by its cover. The place was spacious and airy, with enormous windows, and dark wooden beams crisscrossed the high ceiling. The kitchen was magnificent, with new cabinets over a gleaming stone countertop.

Darby shouted from down the hall, and I wandered over to see what the fuss was about.

"Dibs on this room!" Her hands were clasped to her chest while a bright smile lit up her face. "It's perfect! There's room for my king-sized bed, and my furniture won't be cramped like it is now."

I wagged my finger in her face and smiled, "If this is the biggest room, then I claim it. You may be the 'Princess', but I outrank you, remember?"

"She's right, Darby. You should see the other rooms! They're almost as big. There's a separate laundry room and even a Jacuzzi tub in the bathroom!" Prudence, who was normally the serious, bookish type, let out a girlish squee. "I like it, Bern!"

Darby scampered from the room, eager to claim the next best bedroom. I wandered over to the window. There wasn't much to see outside besides the roof of another building, but that was okay.

"Sooooo? We'll take it?" Prudence sidled up to me. "Please say yes, Bern."

"I just have to see the bathroom and laundry, but if it's as nice as you say, then yes, I think we'll take it."

I shook my head as I wandered through the other rooms. Never in my wildest dreams would I ever have believed I'd be able to afford an apartment in the Soho district! The tiny Bronx apartment had been a stretch on my wages and tips from bar tending. My friends' incomes weren't much better.

Being a Celestial goddess had its perks. And being able to share this with my two best girlfriends totally rocked!

Six

Having settled on paint schemes and a timeline for moving in, we relaxed at the nearby Hilton, sitting on the vast beds with our plates of steak and lobster Thermidor balanced on our laps. The food was as delicious as any restaurant I'd ever been to. And the bottle of champagne on ice was excellent.

Prudence munched on a piece of lobster and then smiled. "This is amazing! Did I call it right, or what? Not only did Saul find us a great place to live, but he's also looking after moving our stuff from the Bronx!"

I grinned back. "That's practically the best part! We never have to see Nosy Natalie again!"

MORTAL ENEMIES (Celtic Knot #3)

It was amazing what a boatload of cash could do to make life sweeter. I looked over at Darby and asked her, "So what will you do with your time, now that you can quit being an office drone?"

She finished the last bite of steak and then took her plate over to the trolley. "I don't know. Definitely celebrate for a bit and then maybe do some travelling. Who knows, if I get bored, maybe I'll take your suggestion and write a book."

"What?" The first two ideas made sense, but Darby a writer? The only time I'd ever seen her with a book was when she stood on one, reaching for something high up. "That wasn't a suggestion, Darb. It was part of my cover story for Saul."

"What? You think I can't do this? I'll be a great writer! I'll show you!" She stood with her arms crossed, challenging me. "So, what are you gonna do now that you don't have to work, Miss Goddess?"

That was a good question. For the first month or so, I'd do whatever I wanted; sleep all day if it suited me, although that would get old pretty quickly. "Maybe I'll write some more songs. There's also charity work; I could volunteer with Habitat For Humanity."

Darby scoffed. "Yeah, right. The songs, sure, but you with a hammer in your hand?" She laughed. Clearing her throat, her expression sobered as she took a seat on the bed next to me. "Do you miss Lugh and Angus, Bern?"

I sighed. "Yeah. And my sister." The truth of it was that Lugh topped the list. How many times had I tried to shut down my memories of him? Too many times to count. I'd have to get over him if I was ever going to accomplish anything with my life.

I looked down at Faellin, as he wolfed down the strip of steak that Pru had given him. He was probably due to go outside. I got up and grabbed my jacket. "C'mon, Faellin! Let's go for a walk."

He wasted no time in jumping up and heading for the

door.

"Want some company?" Pru put her plate away and stretched.

Much as it was nice being with my best friends again, I needed some time alone. Time to just be for a while. "Thanks, Pru, but I've got this. I'd like to be alone, walking along the shoreline for a bit."

"I'd say be careful, but with that beast next to you, no one would dare to bother you." Prudence headed for the bathroom. "I'll take a shower and then try on the pajamas you conjured up."

I waved goodbye to Darby, who was chatting excitedly on her phone, and we headed out the door. As I stepped into the elevator, I couldn't help but think of the morning that Tully and I had ridden in an elevator together, before I'd been ambushed by Morc, Lugh's mortal enemy. I'd hated Tully at first; but after we had spent some time together, everything between us had changed. Just long enough for me to start really liking her.

And then she had died. I rubbed Faellin's head as we descended. I had only known her for a day, and yet I grieved her loss.

Outside, even though dusk was long past, the streetlights and stores illuminated everything nearly as bright as day. At a whine from Faellin, I headed to the park along the river that was only a few blocks away. It was funny. I'd lived in New York City all my life, but this part of the city was not somewhere I visited often. I'm a true New Yorker—I've never even been to the Statue of Liberty!

I practically jogged when Faellin let me know his need to do his business. And for him, that meant a grassy spot, not this concrete. Finally, we arrived at the boardwalk park. I waited next to him as he hunched over. Crap! I'd forgotten to bring a bag with me to clean up after him.

And then I remembered who I was. After glancing over my shoulder to check the area first in case there were people watching, I closed my eyes. And presto, when I opened them there was a green plastic bag on my palm. I held my breath as I scooped up his deposit and then we trotted off to find a garbage container.

We must have walked about half a block when I noticed that ridge of fur spike high on Faellin's back. I tossed the bag into the trash and bent lower, putting my hands on Faellin's head. He was trying to tell me something, and this was the fastest way to get to the bottom of it. Reading the thoughts of animals had been one of the coolest things I'd learned from Flidais.

A low growl erupted in Faellin's throat and a picture of Paul flashed in the dog's head. Paul?

I looked back to where we'd just been, but there were only a few people with their dogs, out for their nightly stroll. I looked Faellin in the eye. "There's nothing there, boy. You must be thinking of seeing him earlier today. I get it. He's a maddening jerk, but he's not here."

We continued on our way and I slowed down to watch a majestic cruise ship ease down the Hudson River. New York really was a beautiful city.

A crack of thunder broke loudly overhead and a flash of lightning zig-zagged across the sky. It wasn't long before the first drops of rain spattered down on my head. Damn. This time I didn't even bother looking around before I conjured up an umbrella big enough to shelter Faellin and me as we headed back to the hotel.

I had to tug on Faellin's leash a few times to keep him moving. He growled repeatedly and tried to break free. There was definitely something or someone around that bothered him. He'd acted the same way when Morc and his brothers had been close by. I'd seen Morc die, though, and the brothers had hightailed it for good, it seemed. So that couldn't be it.

I peered through what had become a torrential downpour of rain by the time I left the park. There were lots of people, like me, hustling to get out of the rain with their hands covering the tops of their heads. I muttered, "I'm not saying you're wrong, Faellin, but we got more important things to worry about than that jerk, Paul. Like not getting soaked to the skin! C'mon!"

We ran across the street and then down the block to our hotel. The cold rain had saturated the bottom of my jeans and Faellin tracked wet prints across the gleaming marble floors in the lobby.

I hoped Pru was out of the shower. Hot water and fleecy PJ's sounded like heaven.

Seven

It was almost four in the afternoon when the last of our furniture was moved into our new apartment. Pru and Darby had gone to the grocery store to stock up while I oversaw where our things were set down.

The mover in charge stopped before heading out the door for the last time. "There's a guy downstairs who tried to follow me in. He said that he's a friend of yours."

I thought at first it might be Lugh, and my heart leapt. But Lugh would just march right in, without asking, so it couldn't be him. "Did he give you his name?"

His forehead wrinkled. "Peter, I think?" He scratched his head and then popped his ball cap on. "Jeeze. I'm terrible with names, lady."

"Could it have been Paul?"

He grinned. "Yeah! That's it. You want me to leave the

door open so he can come in?"

Remembering how Faellin had reacted the night before, and the fact that the superintendent was a real stickler for noise problems, I shook my head. "That's okay, thanks. I'll come down."

I slipped him a freshly minted hundred-dollar bill and smiled. "That's for you and your crew. Have a drink on me."

I'd busied myself with secretly conjuring large sums of cash in while we waited for Saul to give us the keys to our apartment. It had taken a few tries on my part to create perfectly real bills; there were so many security details in printed currency! I eventually figured out how to get it right by holding a hundred dollar bill in one hand while conjuring the copies in the other. I even made sure that the serial numbers were different on each bill. I'd deposited some in the bank to make sure the money was legitimate. If it was good enough for Citibank, it would be good enough for the movers.

"Thanks! If you ever need a mover again, just call us." He handed me a business card.

"Will do!"

I walked out of the apartment and went down to the ground floor. I could see Paul's face plastered to the window at the main entrance, trying to see inside.

Shit! What I didn't need right now was that jerk hanging around and causing trouble that might get us kicked out of the apartment before we'd even spent one night there.

I glared at my ex-boyfriend. "What are you doing here?"

He looked like hell, like he'd slept in the clothes he'd been wearing the day before. The cheesy grin looked worn and tired. He looked agitated.

"I was gonna ask you the same thing! This is quite the improvement over that shithole in the Bronx. How can you afford this place, Bern?" His eyes narrowed, and he thrust his hands in his pockets, trying to look cool but only succeeding in looking awkward and ill at ease.

"You followed me?" I remember Faellin's strange behavior. "You were in the park last night, too! What the hell is up with you? Can't you get it through your tiny brain that we're through?"

"Let me buy you a coffee. If we can just talk for ten minutes, I'll leave you alone afterwards." His head tipped to the side as he begged me.

I gritted my teeth. "Fine, but that's it. You promise to leave me alone afterwards, if I have a coffee with you now?"

"Totally." He lunged towards the door leading into the restaurant and held it open for me.

I stepped carefully around him and took a seat near the window. If Darby and Pru returned early from their trip to the grocery store, I'd ditch him even if before the ten minutes were up. He was already skating on thin ice.

He leaned across the table, holding out his hands and encroaching on my personal space. I scowled at him.

"Bernadette, I've really missed you."

"You said that before, and it's still irrelevant today. You've sunk to a new low, Paul; skulking around in the shadows. What are you now, a stalker?" I sat back, trying to get as far away from him as possible.

"It's not like that, Bernadette."

Oh, God. It was eerily reminiscent of what Angus used to say to me all the time: *'It doesn't work like that, Bernadette.'*

But Paul didn't have a quarter of Angus's class or power, and he was far more manipulative. "Then what is it, if it's not stalking?"

"I was curious, that's all. First, I saw you on the street, going into a gold exchange and now you've moved into a ritzy part of town. Where'd you get the money? You haven't been the same since we went to Ireland. I think you're doing something illegal. That's it, isn't it?"

I rolled my eyes, and then my voice dripped with sarcasm. "Yeah. That's it! You've found me out. I've become an international jewel thief."

He pulled back a bit and then glowered at me. "Nice. I try to help you and you crack funnies. This is no joke, Bernadette. Yeah, I saw you in the park with that mutt last night. You did some things that made me question my own eyesight. Maybe I should tell the cops."

For a moment, I paused, thinking hard. Shit. I'd conjured up a poop bag, but that could be explained easily. But the enormous umbrella might have been a mistake, but it had been dark and rainy. That had been no trick of his eyes, but I wasn't about to tell him that. I snorted, looking down my nose at him. "Actually, it's none of your business anymore. I'm done here. Leave me alone and don't come anywhere near me or my friends again."

Paul ignored me and continued, "You should be careful, Bernadette. Someone might call the cops or the IRS. I can help you, you know. I've got relatives that... well, they specialize in money laundering."

"What the hell are you talking about? Your uncle owns a restaurant, Paul, not some shady operation. Your father's a custodian at the high school. I don't know what your angle is, but I want nothing more to do with you."

I stormed out of the restaurant not even bothering to have that coffee. That he'd made some kind of threat was obvious. The less I had to do with Paul, the better.

***

Still steaming about that jerk I'd been stupid enough to date, I entered the apartment. What the hell did Paul expect me to do? Go running back to him because he threatened me? Totally not going to happen!

I flopped down on the sofa and patted Faellin when he joined me. His big liquid brown eyes looked up at me sadly and I smiled. "Sorry buddy. You were right last night. That jerk was skulking around after us. I should have let you tear into him."

The door opened and Prudence came in, almost eclipsed by the bags of groceries in her arms. Behind her, Darby muttered a complaint about cleaning out the grocery stores; that it wasn't as though they were living in a cabin in Alaska or something!

Pru set the bags on the counter and paused when she looked over at me. "What's wrong? You look like someone pissed in your cornflakes."

I got up and began helping them stock the cabinets and fridge. "That jerk Paul was downstairs when the movers finished up. He's been following us since we left the gold exchange, including last night when I took Faellin for a walk."

Darby's eyes widened, "He's *stalking* you? That's insane! He can't do that. We should call the cops on him."

I stared at her. "And tell them what? He threatened to place a call first! He thinks I'm involved in something illegal... at best."

Pru's head tipped to the side, peering at me. "That's his best guess? What's the worst?"

I took a deep breath and then owned up to my mistake. "Last night, when it started to rain, I... uh... I conjured a huge umbrella to shelter Faellin and me. He saw me do that, apparently. I tried to pass it off that he'd been doing drugs and then there was the downpour of rain, but..."

"Bernadette! You tell us to keep this 'top secret' and then you do something like that out in public?" Prudence shook her head. "To top things off, if he keeps nosing around, he'll see that none of us are working—not that we'd ever be able to afford this place even if we were."

Darby kept putting groceries away. She smiled when she looked at me. "I think you give him too much credit. Who in their wildest dreams would ever guess what Bern's special talents are? I wouldn't believe it either, if I hadn't seen it with my own two eyes."

"I wish that were true, Darby. He's kind of spooked me.

He mentioned going to the IRS, even. That was before he mentioned how 'connected' his family is. He said something about helping me out with laundering cash."

Prudence's mouth pulled to the side, wincing, "Do you think you should get together with him, Bern? Maybe tell him you have just signed a contract for an album, that you have an enormous advance and that your money is none of his business. Hell, even giving him some cash might shut him up."

"No way, Pru! What he's hinting at is blackmail. I'm not scared of Paul! He can go pound sand for all I care." One thing I knew from this confrontation was that I needed to be more careful. The umbrella trick had been a dumb idea.

Maybe, with luck, Paul would second-guess what he'd seen.

Unfortunately, Murphy's law usually trumped dumb luck, as I soon found out.

Eight

We soon settled into our new routine in the apartment. Prudence spent most of the day painting and sketching, sometimes at home or on excursions around the city. Darby spent her time at spas, nail salons and stores. She would take a pic of an article of clothing she thought looked cool, and when she got home, she'd ask me to conjure up the next addition to her wardrobe.

Between practicing my magic and trying to write more songs, I was staying busy. My regular walks with Faellin along the waterfront were a welcome distraction. They also gave me lots of opportunities to shell out cash to the homeless. But even as I did that, I realized that there was so much more that I could accomplish. It might be worthwhile to buy a derelict piece of property and open a soup kitchen or shelter. I'd give it some serious thought.

Soon the call I'd been dreading came through on my phone. Mom. I'd sent her a text a few days before with my new phone number. I took a deep breath and answered in my best and most chipper voice. "Hey Mom! How's—"

"Bernadette! I stopped by your apartment to drop off some pastries when I went into the city today. *You moved?* And I had to find this out from your bitchy landlady? She even asked me for money to cover your last month's rent! What the hell is going on?"

I held the phone away from my ear to keep from going deaf. I could still hear her practically screaming. "You take up with those two guys from Ireland and the next thing I know there are Navy Seals camped outside my house! Then you show up out of the blue in our backyard! I haven't told your father yet about the move, but you owe me an explanation!"

She finally stopped to catch a breath. "Mom! Hang on. I was going to tell you, honest. I'm still getting settled in."

"Where? Where'd you move to? Are you even in New York? Honestly, Bernadette, I never know what to expect next!"

"Yes! I'm in the city. We found an apartment in..." I swallowed hard. "In Soho. It's really nice with hardwood floors and exposed beams and—"

"*SOHO!* How on earth can you afford that? Bernadette, are you selling drugs? Or is it even worse? I wouldn't put it past Darby. The girl's got the morals of an alley cat, but you? I raised you better than that."

"Mom! That's not nice!"

"Do you know what not nice, Bernadette? Moving without telling your own parents." There was a break for about five seconds before her voice became deadly calm. "You will be out here for dinner, TODAY, and we will discuss what's going on with you."

This was followed by dead air. I held the phone out,

looking at it. She'd hung up on me!

This was serious. What the hell was I going to tell her?

***

The smell of pot roast was the first thing I noticed when I entered my parent's home. Looking down at Faellin I saw him lick his lips before we ventured into the kitchen.

I knew it was bad when I saw my father sitting at the end of the table. Normally he would be in the living room catching the sports updates while Mom set the table and served. It usually took at least five times that Mom had to nag him to leave the TV.

"Have a seat, Bernadette." He looked up at me, but a smile never cracked his face.

"I told your father you moved, Bernadette. *To Soho*!" The way she said it was like Soho was a dirty word. Mom brought the pot roast and vegetables to the table and took a seat.

"I'm sorry I didn't tell you guys. I was *going* to, honest." I slipped into the chair across from my father. Why did the stern look in his eyes make me feel like I was nine-years-old? Like the time I'd sneaked cigarettes from his pack, back when he used to smoke.

"You have no plans to return to school and you quit your job. So, how are you paying the rent on a place in Soho? Those places must go for four K a month!" His hands rose to help himself to the roast.

"Actually, five K, if you want to be accurate." I jumped when the bowl slipped from his hand and clattered onto the table.

"*What?* Oh, this is worse than we thought, Lanny." Mom shook her head and wrung her hands over and over.

Dad reached over and stilled Mom's hand. "Let me deal with this, Marion." He turned to me again. "Where are you getting the money for this apartment? And don't tell me it's because Prudence and Darla are chipping in. Neither one of

47

them have great jobs."

"It's *Darby,* Dad. Her name's Darby." Seeing the hard look in Dad's eyes, and the tears in my mother's, I knew it was truth telling time.

Supper was forgotten as I launched into the story, starting with meeting Lugh and Angus at the Moon Pond. I swear my normally vocal mother looked more like a tropical fish, opening and closing her mouth, but for once, words failed her. My dad's face blanched from the florid complexion that had been there when I'd arrived at the house.

It took me three conjuring acts, creating totally crazy objects like a candelabra, a two pound jug of honey and a skateboard for them to believe I hadn't been secretly attending some magician school. There was no way I would try shape-shifting into a cat or penguin in front of them. My dad's heart would never withstand that shock.

Finally, my mother managed one word. "Goddess." She took a deep breath and continued, "You met your biological mother, and her other daughter and now you're a goddess."

I couldn't resist the smart-ass quip after all the times I'd heard both of them lord it over me how wonderful my brother Seth was. "Does that beat having a brother in Harvard med school?"

"Bernadette! This is no joking matter." Dad gave me 'the brook no argument' look. "And what about Seth? What are we supposed to tell *him*?"

I shrugged. "Nothing. Not yet. I haven't seen him in a few months, anyway. It's not like he's gonna see anything different about me. Let's just let this settle for a bit before we include him in this."

"You told your friends even before you let your father and me know. And now you want to keep your brother out of the loop, too! What happened to being a family? Or do you have more loyalty to this sister you just met? To this Lugh character?"

I hadn't pulled punches telling them about Aine's treachery, but Flidais...well; it was obvious that I cared for her. As for Lugh, I really wasn't ready to get into my feelings for him. I was still trying to figure out how I was going to move on. And it had been only a short time we'd been together. Was that what love at first sight was?

I reached for my mother's hand and looked into her eyes. "You are my family. It's why I left Lugh and Otherworld." It wasn't the whole truth, but she didn't need to know that, not now when she was hurting, threatened by my biological family ties.

Dad stood up and popped the pot roast and vegetables into the microwave to reheat them. As he waited, he turned to me. "I hate to say it, but that jerk you once dated has a point, Bernadette. You can't live like you are with no visible means of support. You can for a while, but eventually people are going to take notice. I can help you out with that, setting up a few numbered corporations and off-shore accounts. It's not exactly my field of expertise, but I can do it."

At least my parents were on my side, trying to help. I smiled at him. "If you can work your magic, then I'll work mine. Of course I will pay you for this. Mom's always wanted to go on a cruise. Or maybe get a place in Manhattan. You name it and I can probably make it happen."

"No, no. We're not taking anything from you, Bernadette. It doesn't work like that. It's us who take care of you, remember?" Mom took the bowl of food from Dad and proceeded to help herself.

"That was before, Ma. Before we discovered who I am and what I can do." I helped myself to some dinner and glanced over at her when she murmured.

"Well... I've always wanted to take a Caribbean cruise."

If that was it, I could arrange that '*standing on my head and spittin' nickels*' as Dad had often said when I was younger.

SHELLEY DOREY

A huge stone had been lifted from my back now that my parents knew my secret. Things could only get better.

Famous last words.

Nine

Later, back at my apartment building, I hummed a song as I walked down the hall to my place. I was about to punch in the security numbers to open it when Faellin growled. His head was down, nose sniffing at the floor while a line of fur spiked in the center of his back.

I touched the top of his head, trying to get any clue why he was on high alert. Again, a flash of Paul in his mind coupled with a primal urge to tear my ex's throat out. I punched the buttons on the security lock to get inside. That ass-hat, Paul! Why had Pru and Darby let him in? Maybe I'd let Faellin scare the hell out of him. That would teach him!

When the door opened, I jerked back. A guy stood there, a mountain of flesh in a striped shirt with a seedy jacket thrown over it. But it was the gun in his hand that shot a jolt of terror through me. I grabbed Faellin's collar, holding him back from lunging at the oaf and getting shot.

I knew what that felt like. Except the arrow that had struck me down when I was racing to warn Lugh of Aine's attack, hadn't killed me. A gun at this point blank range would. My heart pounded like a freight train while I stood staring down the barrel of a gun.

The thug stepped to the side, signaling with the gun for me and Faellin to enter. I didn't take my eyes off him as I struggled to keep Faellin at my side, inching by him. One wrong move and it wouldn't matter if I was a Celestial or a panhandler. I'd be dead.

"Bernadette! *Do* something! Take him out with a flamethrower or a bolt of lightning!"

At Darby's shout, I spun around. She and Prudence huddled close together on the sofa while a gray-haired man behind them had a gun pointed at Prudence's head!

My blood froze. If only it was as simple as throwing a bolt of lightning. Sure, I could conjure that up to fight these two thugs, but not before their guns would go off. In those seconds it would take to imagine a weapon, they would have used theirs.

Movement to the side caught my attention. Seeing Paul strolling from the kitchen area carrying a glass of water, my jaw clenched tight.

"Hey Bernadette! Nice for you and that mangy mutt to finally join us. Allow me to introduce my uncle Antonio." He handed the glass to the old guy, who nodded his thanks. "I told my uncle about your upscale lifestyle even though none of you gals have a job anymore."

He kept walking over to where I stood. "He was really interested how you have been able to pull that off." He smiled and glanced back at my friends. "But thanks to Darby, we've learned that you can do all *kinds* of amazing tricks."

Darby's eyes widened, and she yelled, "I'm *sorry*, Bern! They threatened Pru. If I didn't say something they would have broken Pru's jaw."

I looked closer when Prudence's head turned slightly. Oh, my god! It was hard to even see her eyeball in the puffy swelling of flesh around it. They'd hit her!

But before I could say anything, Faellin strained against my grip, snarling, and showing teeth at the thug standing just a few feet away. There was no doubt that he wouldn't hesitate to shoot my dog if Faellin attacked.

"Stop, Faellin! Enough." I didn't bother answering Paul, but looked at the old man instead. "Let me put my dog in my room. The neighbors or the Super are gonna hear him, and then they'll be banging on the door. If you let me do that, we'll talk and clear this up."

The thug close to me snickered, "A bullet in the dog's brain would settle him down. Then, you'd be sure to want to have a little talk."

"Don't let her do *anything*, Uncle Antonio! It's a trick! You heard her friend. She's liable to come back with a machine gun or something."

For the first time, the old guy spoke. His voice was raspy, barely audible as he stepped closer to Prudence, putting a hand on her shoulder. "Quiet, Paul. I'm certain that your girlfriend will play nice. There's no need for anymore violence." I saw Pru wince when his hand on her shoulder tightened. "Isn't that right, Bernadette?"

Not trusting myself to answer, I walked Faellin to my bedroom and admonished him. "Quiet! It's okay, Faellin." All the while, my mind raced to find something I could do to end this nightmare. Shape shifting into a panther would take precious moments, and even if I pulled it off, that would be no match for a gun. And if I managed to produce a weapon, then Prudence or Darby might be hurt in the crossfire. I was new to this Celestial stuff, not able to do these things without concentrating my mind.

There was no other way than to see what the hell they wanted from me.

53

When I walked back to the living room, I hissed at the uncle. "First, I'm getting some ice for my friend's eye. No tricks, I promise."

Again he shrugged. He was holding all the cards, so why shouldn't he?

I squeezed in next to Pru and put the ice wrapped in a tea towel to her eye. Her hand rose to keep it there. Scowling at the uncle, my voice was steadier than I'd ever thought possible, given the circumstances. "I'm afraid there's been a misunderstanding here, Antonio. I inherited money from a relative in Ireland. I don't know what Darby told you, but it was an inheritance. I just returned from my father's house. He's a lawyer." I let that sink in and watched for any reaction, but only a faint smile lifted his thin lips. "My father is handling the estate. It's all very legal."

At a slight nod from the old man, his thug thundered across the room. When he reached Darby, his fist drew back.

"Stop! Don't hurt her!"

The thug glanced at the old man.

Paul shook his head and blurted, "That's B.S. Where'd the money come from? I'd call Darby crazy with that outlandish tale of you being some kind of magician or something, if I hadn't seen you pull a golf umbrella out of *thin air*."

Paul started for the couch, but I held my hand high, like a traffic cop, stopping him. "No closer, you weasel!" I looked up at the uncle. "What do you want from me?"

Antonio sauntered slowly to the chair across from us and nodded to his henchman. Immediately the thug stood behind Pru, a threatening world of hurt, just waiting for the word to continue the beating.

"Is this true? Can you make things appear out of thin air? How about money?" He sat back, but his eyes never left my face, examining me like I was his next meal—more like a meal ticket.

MORTAL ENEMIES (Celtic Knot #3)

I sighed and nodded, taking Darby's hand when her fingers sought mine. I could see why she'd told them everything. These guys would stop at nothing. Paul hadn't been boasting when he'd said that his uncle was connected. I had a funny feeling that laundering money wasn't the only crooked stuff he was into. He was old and kind of jowly to be a gangster, but what had I expected? Al Pacino?

"Prove it. Make a hundred-dollar bill appear in your hand." The old man's hoarse whisper was the only sound in the room. All eyes were on me.

I had to pretend that this was harder than it actually was. Sure, I was buying time, but what else could I do? That old tale of Jack and the beanstalk and the giant with the goose laying the gold eggs raced through my head. Except in this case, I was that goose.

Standing up, I made a show of closing my eyes and holding my hands out, palms up. I even muttered some gibberish. My eyes opened, and I looked at the uncle. "This isn't easy. It doesn't help that some clown has a gun threatening me and my friends. Tell him to put it away."

Again with a mere glance at his thug, the gun was slipped into the back of the guy's pants. My eyes closed, and I strained, even managing to tremble a bit as I played this out.

"She's stallin'. Uncle Antonio. I saw her get the umbrella to appear just like that." Paul snapped his fingers.

"Quiet! Try again, Bernadette. But if you're screwing around with this, I'm afraid that your friends are gonna pay the price. And that'll be just for starters."

Again, I closed my eyes and waited for just a minute before picturing a hundred-dollar bill. I didn't need to see it to know from the gasps coming from Paul and the thug it had worked.

"Good! That's much better, Bernadette. Now try a few gold bars. If you can make that appear, then I think we'll all get along. I have no wish to cause anyone discomfort."

I stared at the old man with narrow eyes. "Okay, but first

you need to let my friends go. They're innocent. This is between you and me."

"Don't do it, Uncle Antonio. They'll go to the cops or the FBI. You can't trust those two skanks." Paul stepped over closer to Darby, glaring down at her.

"What did I tell you, Paul? You've done well, my boy, but leave the heavy thinking to me." The old man smiled at Darby and Pru like they were long lost buddies. "These young ladies won't go to the police. What could they tell them? That their friend is some kind of magic creature who creates things out of thin air? They'd be laughed out of the station house. And even if some fool believed them enough to investigate, Bernadette would be arrested for counterfeiting. That is, if she wasn't seized by the CIA to try to dissect her. This kind of power could come in pretty handy in their line of work."

Antonio nodded to Darby and Pru. "You may go to your rooms. When your friend gets me the gold, you can leave the building. But, know this. I've got guys watching. This little secret is between us. You don't spill the beans and everyone benefits. We can all celebrate your friend's gifts."

I watched Darby and Prudence rise. Both of them looked over at me before they raced from the room. Part of me was relieved, but another part wanted to rip these guys into shreds — especially, Paul.

Again, I hesitated while conjuring up the gold bullion. In the best of times it would take a few moments, getting a good picture in my head, but not nearly as slow as I was taking now. It might be the only edge I had. There was no one here who could help me; not the police or anyone in the government. I couldn't risk my friends or Faellin being hurt or even killed by these thugs.

After picturing the gold ingots, my hands sank lower when two heavy bars of gold appeared.

"Amazing! This is simply astounding!" The old man's eyes lit up, staring at the gold. He smiled at me, "What else can you do, Bernadette?"

Ten

My face tightened, and I sneered, "What else can I *do*? Two gold bricks aren't enough for you?" I blew out a fast sigh. "Look, I did what you asked. Now it's your turn. Let my friends go."

He lifted a finger, and immediately his thug walked over to the bedroom door. He tapped it a couple times before he opened it. "Youse can go now. But keep your traps shut or it'll be the last thing you ever say. Got it?"

Prudence and Darby appeared in the doorway, looking over at us. I nodded to them. "Go! I'll call you later. This is my problem to deal with."

Prudence shook her head, "No, Bern! We're not leaving you here with these guys." Beside her, a wide-eyed Darby just stared.

"Please. I don't want to worry about you. Trust me, I can

handle this." I even managed a smile that felt more like a grimace on my lips. But I couldn't risk them getting hurt anymore than they already had.

Darby took Pru's hand and led the way across the apartment to the door. She turned before leaving. "If you hurt Bernadette, then all bets are off. We'll go to the F.B.I. or the C.I.A. or someone to make you pay!"

The old man waved his hand as if shooing a fly away. When the door closed, he smiled at me. "I don't believe all the goddess mumbo jumbo, but it's clear you've got some kind of supernatural talent that you can do this. What other talents do you possess?"

I knew that his question wasn't motivated by greed this time. No. He was wondering if I posed some kind of threat to his physical wellbeing. If he only knew. I was glad that I'd never told my friends about shape shifting or being able to read minds. I could only hope that Darby had left out telling him about my transitioning through time and space.

"What other talents? Well, I sing. Wonderful things happen when I sing." My eyes narrowed and I smiled. Oh Yeah. They would soon find out the power of my song.

We're time and worlds apart
Yet still you're in my heart.
The streets I walk alone
Never to lead me to your home

At the same time that I was singing, watching Antonio's face become looser, stifling a yawn, my mind was thinking of what I could use to tie them up with. I'd seen murderous gods zonk out after I sang to them. These small-time hoods wouldn't stand a chance.

What I thought would bring
solace
Sheds light on an empty morass

I sneaked a peek over at Paul, who had sunk into the chair across from me. His head fell to the side while his eyelids had grown heavier. A look at his uncle showed his mouth had loosened and a dribble of drool glistened on his lips. It was difficult to keep my voice even as I continued singing. It was working!

*I close my eyes and see you
there
The two of us together without
a care
Do you see me in your dreams
Or is life as empty as it seems
My earnest joy in this time and
space
T'would only exist if all were
erased
Your world and mine are as
night and day
But in my dreams, together we
lay
Each dawning morn awakes
with pain
All my thoughts and desires in
vain*

The soft thud behind me told me that the guy with the gun was out too. From the nasal snores coming from Paul's uncle, it was plain he was sleeping like a babe. I tiptoed to the back of the sofa and seeing the thug lying on his side; I reached down to pluck the gun from the back of his pants.

He stirred, and my chest froze in my chest. His mouth opened, and he smacked his lips before a faint smile appeared. He was definitely in la-la land. I slid the gun into my pocket and walked around the sofa and the chair where Antonio was snoring.

As I moved, my hands extended, picturing a jail cell that would keep these guys here to give me and my friends enough time to get far away. My foot clanged against something metal and I opened my eyes. Great! I'd managed to include myself in the ten by ten foot cell. Once more I tried and this time when I opened my eyes there was an open door in the cell. I slipped out and closed it behind me. I quickly conjured a lock for the door.

Feeling better with the thugs inside the cage and disarmed, I crept over to let Faellin out. "Shush. C'mon boy." I had to practically drag him out. He tugged, trying to get at the guys sleeping in the living room. But at least he hadn't barked or let out any growls.

When I was outside, I pulled my phone from my purse and hit the button to get Prudence. Stepping inside the elevator, I knew going to the front door wasn't an option, not with Antonio's guys watching the building. I hit the button going to the basement level.

"Bernadette! Are you okay?"

My eyes closed for a moment, hearing Pru's voice and Darby in the background. "Yes. I managed to put them all to sleep and escaped. Where are you?"

"We're in a coffee shop down the street. How'd you get them to sleep?" Pru asked.

"Never mind that now. I'll tell you later. We've got to find a place to hide for a while. I'll try to find a back entrance in this building that's hopefully clear of Antonio's guys. But what about you? Do you think you can give these guys the slip?"

It was Darby who answered. I could picture the two of them huddled over Pru's phone. "For sure! We'll slip out a back door as well. But where will we meet?"

"Over in Queens. Go to the Holiday Inn on Hyde Street. But take separate routes. Darby, you take the subway and Pru, you can take a bus. With any luck, there won't be two guys tailing you now. I'm taking a taxi so I'll be there ahead of you."

"Why can't I take a cab?" Darby's voice bordered on

being whiny. But it was Pru who settled the matter.

"She's got the cash, Darb. And she's the one they're after. You'll be fine."

The elevator dinged, and I arrived in the basement level. When I stepped out the smell of garbage hit me full in the face. Eeew. I saw a door labeled Utility Room and another door across the hall. That must be the Super's unit. I held my nose and entered the Utility room. There had to be outside access for the garbage to be put out. I spied the door and Faellin and I raced for it.

When we were outside we both panted, trying to get the stink out of our noses from the garbage bins. I sank down next to Faellin, a plan forming in my head. I couldn't take a chance that I'd be spotted when I emerged from behind the building.

I held Faellin's head, looking into his eyes. "Stay with me, boy. We're both about to get enough exercise to last us a week." I closed my eyes and pictured Faellin, getting my head into becoming a dog like him. It would still be risky running the streets of New York as a wolfhound, but maybe after a few blocks I could transition back. The thugs—if they were watching—would never suspect two dogs sidling out from behind the building.

The familiar trembling and twitching as my body changed was a relief. The times I'd done this before had always felt a bit weird, but not now. The smells assaulting my nose were the first sign that I was now a dog. I opened my eyes and there was Faellin staring back at me, his tail wagging.

It was funny. In all the time since I'd learned that I could do this, I'd wanted to run alongside Faellin to see and hear what he experienced. It took a visit from Paul and his horrible family to make it happen. When Faellin started sniffing my nose and then going around to sniff my posterior, I yelped. That was a little too familiar to my liking.

I took off, trotting at first until I came to the street.

MORTAL ENEMIES (Celtic Knot #3)

There were people out walking and a cop was stationed at the corner. That could be a problem, but I had to take the chance. I let out a low whine and rounded the corner of the building, heading up the street. I could hear Faellin's heavy paws thudding behind me as we walked. Staying as close to the buildings as possible, we broke out into a run.

A young couple staggering from their evening at a bar pointed to us and yelled. "Look! It's like werewolves in London, except this is the Big Apple!" They broke out laughing, weaving even more.

The smell of alcohol wafted in the air and I had to dodge to keep from hurtling into the guy, but we soon passed them. Just one more block and we'd dart into an alley for me to transition back. It was a *long* city block. A middle-aged man with a miniature poodle came to a dead top seeing us bounding towards him. The poodle let out a yelp and then was scooped up into the guy's arms.

"Hey! Where's a cop when you need one? Someone! Get those dogs outta here!"

"Yap!" Faellin let out a bark and I turned my head to see him about to go back.

"No! Faellin!" But it came out as an even louder yap than his. But it was enough to get his attention. He fell in line behind me once more.

But the cop had noticed us after the guy yelled. He pounded the pavement, trying to catch us while he yelled into his radio. "Request Animal Control. Two large dogs are on the loose, running down Broadway near Spring."

Shit! We were just about at Prince Street. Spying the sign of a subway station, we raced down the stairs. There were two guys, homeless from the looks of them, ambling next to a bundle of blankets on the floor. I darted behind a pillar and closed my eyes. It was hard to concentrate, to get my mind to the place it needed to be to transition back into my own body. I could hear the cop coming down the stairs and in the distance, the rumbling of a train.

My body twitched and jerked, and for the first time a pain shot up my spine. "Oow!" I opened my eyes and saw my hand. I had transitioned so fast that my body hurt! Faellin looked at me with big, sad eyes. He'd enjoyed running with me. "Sorry, boy!"

When the train pulled up to the platform, I herded Faellin into the car and got in behind him. As the train pulled away, I saw the cop who had been chasing us staring back. But he was too late. I'd get out at the next station and grab a cab. I'd given the thugs and the police the slip.

Whew! I only hoped that Pru and Darby had also been successful. If not, we were in a world of trouble.

Eleven

Twenty minutes later, Faellin and I walked into the same hotel where I'd stayed with Lugh and Angus. I'd picked it as a meeting place because they were pet friendly. Having just been a wolfhound like Faellin, I had a new appreciation for that policy.

I was just finishing paying and doing the room booking when Prudence bolted through the door. "Bernadette!" She rushed over to my side and hugged me. Seeing her puffy, black eye made my stomach tighten. That black eye was all my fault.

I finished scribbling my name on the form and grabbed the key cards before turning to her again. "Everything okay?"

She looked up from where she bent, rubbing Faellin's head. "Yes. Aside from the shiner, I'm fine. I didn't see anyone following us when we left the cafe. How 'bout you?"

I shook my head. There was no way I'd get into the shape shifting thing with her. It was better for everyone that I kept this to myself. "Fine! If there was anyone there, we gave them the slip." I blinked a few times, listening to myself. Since when had I become an underworld figure talking about giving someone the 'slip'?

We took the elevator up to the ninth floor and found our room at the end of a long hallway. When the door closed behind us, I breathed a long sigh of relief. We were safe for a little while at least. I pulled the gun from my bag for good measure.

"Darby should be here soon. But it wouldn't hurt to call her to see that she's okay." Pru pulled her phone out and clicked on Darby's contact info.

I watched her and felt my gut tighten as I waited. She should have answered by now. When Pru huffed a sigh and then left a message for Darby to call ASAP, it only increased the feeling of dread.

Prudence looked over at the gun lying on the dresser. "Do you know how to use that thing?" She wandered over and picked it up, looking down the sights as she aimed it at a lamp. She pushed a button on the side and a clip of ammo dropped out from the handle. She tugged on the top of the barrel, slid it back and a bullet popped out. She picked the bullet up and inserted it into the top of the clip from the gun. She peered down inside the gun. "It's safe now," she said, putting the gun and the clip on the night table.

I grinned, watching her. "I don't know the first thing about guns, but it looks like you know your way around one."

"I took a few lessons and did some target shooting. Yeah, I'm not too bad with one." She looked over at me. "So this is the goon's gun, I presume. You never told me how you were able to put them to sleep."

I flopped down on the bed. "My singing. Remember, I

awakened Lugh with my song? It's one of my gifts."

"You might have to sing me a lullaby after what we just went through. I'm wound up tighter than a spool of thread." Her fingers went to her eye and touched the swollen flesh gingerly. "It probably looks worse than it feels."

I didn't have the heart to agree with her. I looked at my cell phone, checking the time. It was ten minutes after eleven. "I'll give Darby another twenty minutes but if she's not here by then, we'll have to assume the worst, that Antonio's guys got her. We'll have to leave this hotel, Pru."

She nodded. "Exactly what I was thinking. I wish she'd call to let us know if she's okay."

At the tap on the door, I was off the bed in a shot. But Pru was ahead of me, grabbing the gun. She slid the clip back in and ratcheted the weapon. "Who's there?"

"It's me! Darby! Let me in!"

Pru looked through the peephole and then opened the door. Darby burst in, giving Pru a wide berth when she caught sight of the gun. "Whoa! Where'd you get *that*?"

"Did anyone follow you, Darby?"

"No! But the subway at night! What a carnival that is! How 'bout you two? Are we safe here?"

"For a while, we are. As long as no one saw us. I'm going to call my folks to let them know. The next trick Antonio might pull is to threaten them." I took out my phone and made the call. It rang for about ten times before my father's voice grumbled.

"Bernadette? Do you know what time it is?" And then his words came out fast. "What's wrong? Are you all right?"

I spent the next twenty minutes trying to convince him I was safer where I was than at his house. That is, once I'd convinced him that calling the police wasn't an option. Not yet, at any rate. Whatever we could tell the cops would only make matters worse.

I just needed time to figure out a plan to deal with these small time mafia thugs. Shouldn't be too hard. They were dealing with a goddess after all.

Okay. A naive goddess, but a goddess nonetheless.

Twelve

A fter the third day of hiding out in the hotel, only broken by quick walks to the parking lot for Faellin to do his business. We were all getting stir crazy and snapping at each other.

Darby looked up from her task of painting her toenails for the umpteenth time, this time a shade of purple that matched Pru's shiner. "I'd almost rather be back at my job at the office. No offense gals, but watching you two play Scrabble is boring. Where's the life of leisure and riches that we were supposed to have? Can't you do something about all this, Bernadette?"

Darby continued her litany of complaints. "Maybe we should ditch this country. We could fly to Europe or Australia even. Why are we stuck in this hotel?"

Pru scowled when she looked over at her. "Oh, so you

have a passport? Funny, I forgot mine the last time I was in *France!*"

Yeah, hearing Pru's sarcasm underscored the fact that soon we'd bite each other's heads off. "Look. This is my problem, okay? I'll scope things out. Maybe go around the block looking for any thug who could be one of Antonio's guys. If the coast is clear, we'll go out for dinner or something to break the monotony."

Pru's eyes closed for a moment, and then she snorted. "You don't think with the flaming red hair and this miniature horse at your side, you won't draw attention if they're around? At least leave Faellin here."

But I was one step ahead of her, already scooping my hair up and securing it with an elastic.

Darby looked up, "Try a baseball cap, too. Conjure one up, Bern and tuck your hair under it. A pair of dark glasses won't hurt and a black hoodie, too."

I smiled over at her before I closed my eyes to get my costume ready. "If all else fails, I'll hold up a Seven Eleven. God knows, I'm dressed for it." It took only about twenty seconds before the rest of my outfit was done.

I gave Faellin a pat on his head. "Not this time, boy. I'll be back soon and then maybe all of us can go to the park for a bit."

"Yap!" The tail wagging stopped and then he sunk down onto the floor, He wouldn't even look at me. Yeah. We all needed a break, even Faellin.

I took one last look in the mirror before going to the door. Not a lock of my hair showed. My own mother wouldn't recognize me. It felt good to step out into the hallway and ride the elevator down to the main floor. It's funny how you take freedom for granted until it's gone. Much like everything else, I guess. Even Lugh. I'd give anything to see him again, if only for an hour.

Outside, it was chilly but dazzling with the sun cascading rays over the street. I looked both ways before deciding on heading toward Astoria. There were people out and about, hustling to make the train or just ambling slowly along arm in arm, or with a dog on a leash.

As I walked along the street, I considered Darby's comment to travel. How hard could it be to conjure up a few passports and leave the country? I'd managed to create cash that passed the test at a bank. It would be way safer roaming the streets of London or Paris than hanging out, looking over my shoulder in case Antonio's goons were around.

But so far, scanning the area, it was just normal people walking around. Spying a grocery store on the next block, I decided to treat myself with a chocolate bar. Maybe I'd get a few for my friends.

But before I could cross the street, two guys appeared at each side of me. Their hands gripped my arms and my heart jumped into my throat. When a dark limousine pulled up to the curb, my eyes opened wide, and I tried to yank myself free of their grip. But they were *big*! I mean almost as big as Lugh! "Hel—" My cry got squelched by a sweaty paw.

They frog-marched me to the car, while my legs kept striding in the air. The door opened, and they flung me inside. I'd barely landed when the car pulled away from the corner, speeding down the street.

I managed to push myself up from where I'd landed on the floor. My mouth fell open seeing the elderly man sitting there, next to the window.

He smiled and extended a hand to help me. "Bernadette Adelson. I finally tracked you down." In the expensive sharkskin suit and manicured nails, he was a far cry from Antonio's ilk. Even the cologne and neatly trimmed, white hair oozed money. Not to say anything of the limo and leather seats. All of this went through my head in a flash.

"Who are you? How do you know my name?" I brushed my hoodie off and then sat on the seat. Until I knew if he was a savior or crook, I'd watch him carefully. He looked kindly enough, but looks could be deceiving.

"My name is Wesley Bloomstein." He glanced out the window and smiled. "I own many of these properties you see outside. Even the hotel where you and your friends are staying is in my portfolio of investments. I know of your recent trouble with Antonio Savatini. He's a buffoon. A capable person, but a nasty buffoon nonetheless."

"You're telling me?"

He nodded. "Yes, but everyone has their purpose, no?"

I stared at him silently as the creeping realization settled into my bones. I sensed his thoughts which were even more reprehensible than Antonio's. He gloated inwardly that he'd secured a prize, like me. But I couldn't let on that I saw right through him. My telepathic gift was another secret best not shared with this rich thug. Even as he continued in a friendly conversation, like he was talking to a favorite niece, I saw the connection to Antonio.

"Antonio is an associate... well, more like an employee actually. When it became known that he was trying to trade some gold bullion, I made some enquiries." He chuckled. "Antonio's type is quite close with their families. But the younger generation isn't quite so loyal. His nephew, Paul, was only too happy to let me know where that gold originated."

His gnarled finger lifted, and he tried to put it under my chin, but I jerked away from the old reptile. Undeterred, he continued. "Imagine my surprise when he told me you produced it out of *thin air.*"

My eyes narrowed when I glared at him. "What do you want? You don't have *enough* money that you want me to create more for you? You're a greedy—"

"*Not money!* I couldn't spend what I have in ten lifetimes. Not even a hundred. No, Bernadette. Anyone who can do what you do can create so much more than that. I'm talking about *life*, here, Bernadette! New life!"

"Life! You mean *youth.*" I knew I was right even looking

at the way his eyes glinted. But I'd also read his thoughts. This old geezer had everything that this world could provide him with except longevity. Somehow, he felt that I could give him that.

"You're smarter than your boyfriend gave you credit for." His smile fell. "Yes, I want youth. But there's much more. Your kind needs to reproduce, to create more like you. That's the only way this planet will survive. With food shortages, war, climate change, we're at risk of annihilation. I intend to harness the solutions with you at my side. We'll control everything."

I couldn't help the look of revulsion that crept into my face. He was literally turning my stomach with all this talk of him being some kind of world savior. What was worse, he absolutely believed it. "What are you? Some kind of Dr. Evil like in an Austin Power movie? You're insane if you think that I'm going to ever have anything to do with you."

Bloomstein, or Weinstein or whatever the hell his name was, leaned forward and tapped the shoulder of his guy riding shotgun in the front. He took the phone from his henchman and held it out for me to see.

Oh my God! I gasped seeing my mother and father hunched on the sofa. From the disheveled clothes my father wore to the wild-eyed look in Mom's eyes, they had been attacked. The phone flipped to show a blond-haired giant grinning at me. They'd taken my parents hostage to get me to cooperate! But it wasn't just my parents. My friends were back at the hotel with Faellin.

Bloomstein's hotel.

Thirteen

The phone went dark and for a moment; I sat frozen with terror. My parents were not only innocent bystanders; they were getting on in years. Dad was already in his sixties and Mom wasn't far behind him. If anything happened to them, my world would break. I might as well die myself.

I had to think of something, *anything* to save them. If it was just me to worry about, I'd conjure up something to disable the old man; like a fireball hovering over my palm. The threat of it had worked on the insufferable demi-god girls in Otherworld. But now it wouldn't be a *threat* I'd level, at this old reptile. I'd gladly set that ten K suit he wore *ablaze* with him still in it, right after I flew some flames at his driver and goon.

But it wasn't that easy, not with my parents held hostage. I had to pretend to cooperate if they were going to get out of this mess unscathed. "Okay. I get the picture, Bloomstein. I'll do whatever it is you want, just don't hurt my mom and dad."

He handed the phone back to the dark-haired thug in the front seat. Smiling, he turned to me. "I have no wish to hurt anyone, Bernadette. In fact, the very opposite is true. For a person to have a gift like yours and not use it for the betterment of mankind would truly be a crime."

I sneered at him. "Kind of like kidnapping me, and threatening my parents isn't a crime? Kind of like that?"

"You aren't seeing the big picture, Bernadette." His eyes became narrow slits. "Show me. I'm still trying to wrap my head around the fact that you can create something out of nothing. Although Paul was very emphatic that he witnessed it, along with two other people."

"You make me sound like a trained seal, performing tricks. It's not that easy." It totally was, even if I wasn't nearly as fast at doing it as my older sister. I wished I'd had more time to practice this.

Without hesitation, Bloomstein tapped his thug's shoulder, signaling for the phone again.

The casual threat made my chest tighten. "Stop! Look, I'll try, okay?" I looked outside the car window, seeing that we were now crossing the Whitestone Bridge, leaving Queens. "Where are you taking me?"

But his only response was to sit back in the seat, eyeing me like a hawk. There was no way I'd be able to delay this by getting him to talk. I closed my eyes and the first thing I pictured was a knife to plunge into his thigh. Crap! That would make my parents suffer even more. But there was no way I would make this easy on Bloomstein and his minions.

At the vibration in my palm, I jerked back. With a flick of my hand, I unleashed a swarm of bees! The car swarmed with them, attacking Bloomstein and the other two guys.

"Hey!" the driver's hand left the wheel to brush off a couple bees that landed on his neck. The other goon's hands whooshed through the air, trying to fend off the bugs, while Bloomstein screamed. The bees completely ignored me, focusing their anger (my anger, I guess) on this crew. The car swerved, almost bouncing off the car in the next lane. I hung onto the hand rest as we careened across the bridge. With any luck, some highway cop would stop the car and arrest them.

"Make it stop! Open the damned windows!" Bloomstein's cheek showed a few red welts and his hand still had a couple bees clinging to it. "Give me the phone!"

The open windows sucked most of the bees out, but there were still a handful crawling on the seat ahead of me. When Bloomstein's guy thrust the phone up over his shoulder, I grabbed it and tossed it out. There was no way that call was getting through, a call that would ultimately hurt Mom and Dad.

"You stupid girl! You don't think I can't make that call?" Bloomstein hair whipped back from his face to show several more stings on his forehead. He fished his own cell from his pocket and held it in his fist, glaring at me.

By this time we'd left the bridge and the driver had pulled the car to the side of the road. Both the driver and the guy in the front bolted from the car, leaving the doors wide open. Now was my chance! I grabbed the phone from Bloomstein's hand and tossed it on the floor next to my foot. Just a few quick stomps of my foot and the thing was disabled.

The thug from the front seat opened my door, and his hand went around my throat. His eyes glared at me while steadily increasing the pressure on my windpipe.

When my hand lifted, to claw his fingers away, there was a razor-sharp knife in it. I could hardly believe it myself, but I quickly got over the surprise, slashing his hand.

A stream of blood flew over my chest when he yanked his hand back, holding it in his other. My heart raced as I spun to face Bloomstein, gripping the knife in my fist. "Back off! I swear I'll kill you, if you don't. You're going to drive to my parents' house and you will free them."

The old man's flinty eyes left the knife to look to where the driver had gone. "Eric!"

But when the driver knelt over the front seat, he held his cell phone in his hand. He shoved it over the seat to show me the screen. My heart sank seeing the blond thug standing over my father with the muzzle of a gun pressing Dad's temple.

A sharp pain at the back of my neck made me jerk. At first I thought it was a bee, but then the dark-haired thug's voice followed. "Drop the knife." That bastard had injected me with something!

Bloomstein's face tightened, and he let out a long breath. "Quite the impressive display, Bernadette. Now do as you're told and your parents live to see another day. If you have any plans to unleash any more hornets or some other pestilence, I'd advise you to reconsider."

The knife slipped from my hand onto the seat. As long as these guys had my parents, the only thing I could do was cooperate and wait for an opportunity. I blinked a few times when the insides of the car swirled. A look over at Bloomstein showed his face kind of melting and chin elongating. My head slumped forward and my eyes closed. After that, everything went dark.

***

A nudge on my shoulder brought me back to consciousness.

"Hey! Wake up."

I shrugged the hand away and creaked my eyes open. Bloomstein's thug bent over, facing me. His cheek and eyelid were swollen and a couple red circles showed where the bees had got him. He was huge and his flattened nose showed he'd seen many a fight.

When I tried to stand I immediately felt the restraints. They had secured my feet and wrists to the back of a chair with some kind of tie that almost cut off the blood flow.

Even wiggling my fingers was impossible. Shit! They'd bound my hands in some kind of gloves. Nausea in my stomach tightened my throat, and I gagged a few times. "Water. I need some water." It had to be the effects of whatever drug they'd given me.

"Of course, my dear." It was then that I noticed Bloomstein in the room. He poured a glass from a pitcher on the table next to him and walked over to me. Holding it to my lips he murmured, "Midazolam sometimes produces mild nausea when it wears off. You'll be fine in an hour or so. I wish you hadn't forced me to use it."

I swallowed a big gulp and then turned my head. "I didn't force you to do anything. Unlike what you're doing to me! I have friends who will miss me, you know. They'll go to the police and you'll be arrested for this."

He tsked a couple of times. "Darby? Prudence? I don't think they'll be making any calls, anytime soon. They're guests in my hotel under lock and key. If you promise to cooperate, they'll be freed. All it takes is a phone call, just like that call regarding your parents."

I'd known that my friends were in danger, but hearing it made my gut sink. Bloomstein had covered all bases to get me to do his bidding. "What is it you want me to do?"

I looked around the room, taking in the fact that the walls were ceramic tile and that there was a long stainless steel counter running the length of the far wall. It was some kind of lab, judging by the microscopes, the small trays of vials and beakers.

"Do? Actually, very little. We've taken blood samples and will run some tests to isolate any particles that may be out of the norm. After that, a CAT scan and MRI. There has to be some physical element to how you're able to 'create'." Bloomstein pulled up a chair and sat a few feet away, facing me.

"So, I'm basically a lab rat." I had no idea if he'd ever find any physical element to what made me what I am. I'd been to doctors and even had my tonsils out when I was thirteen. If there'd been anything off about me, they would have uncovered it then. My power had only manifested when I was around Lugh and Angus. And I was pretty sure that Moon Pond in Ireland had helped as well.

Bloomstein chuckled. "Hardly a lab rat, not after what I saw today. Why, you're a walking, talking 3D printer when you put your mind to it." He leaned closer. "Bernadette, we will isolate whatever gives you this power. It may even show in your brain waves. But in the meantime, the process to clone your cells and recreate you has already begun."

"So if you've got all this in place, why do you need me here? Aside from my not having you arrested?"

"No one would ever arrest me, Bernadette. I have a team of the best legal minds in the country to look after my interests. The best medical and scientific researchers as well; to investigate how you do what you do. But I still need you to cooperate on more tests. I want to do cognitive, psychological and psychic evaluations."

"Still sounding like a lab rat to me. So once you've done all these tests, will you let me go? You'll have what you need, so why keep me?" But I knew there was no way he'd ever agree to that. He wanted to corner the *Bernadette* market. He couldn't risk any other psycho billionaire getting their hands on me. These guys didn't amass billions of dollars because they were great humanitarians, no matter what Bill Gates and company want you to believe.

He stood up. "We'll discuss that down the road. In the meantime, I'd like you to join me for dinner." He nodded to something behind me and two women along with two guys in green scrubs stepped forward.

"You are going to be released and accompanied while you shower. Your hands will however remain in their protective shields. I don't want another swarm of bees attacking my staff. If you resist, I'm afraid you will be sedated again. Let's try to make this a civil if not a friendly endeavor, shall we?"

With that, he left me in the hands of his team. I wouldn't even get the chance to see if the shields on my hands worked. It looked like he was never going to let me go unguarded, not even having a shower.

Fourteen

They escorted me down a long corridor before we entered an elevator. A glance at the two guys next to me showed that if they were medical personnel, they must have gone through school on a football scholarship. They were masses of muscles that I would have no chance to overcome on my own. I don't know what those gloves were made of, but somehow, with my hands in them, my magical abilities felt out of reach. The light on the elevator flipped through a few numbers as it ascended before coming to a stop.

When I stepped outside, it was like entering another world. Paintings and sculptures adorned the wide hallway on each side, while a Persian runner cushioned my feet. He'd also made sure that I had new clothes, even though blue surgical scrubs hardly qualified as the height of fashion.

They led me through a door where a gleaming oak table was set with a flower centerpiece and fine china. At the end of the table was Bloomstein, casually dressed in a cashmere cardigan and dark pants. He rose from his chair and pulled out a chair for me to sit next to him.

A woman in a uniform wheeled in an array of dishes and set them on the table. Bloomberg took a seat and smiled at me. "I hope you like lamb but if you prefer seafood, there's shrimp and scallops. Would you care for some wine?"

Not waiting for me to answer, he took the bottle that had been set down and poured two generous glasses. "I was married at one time but Evelyn died, unfortunately. She contracted a virus while vacationing, and there was nothing that could be done to save her."

"That's very sad for you." There was no use in antagonizing him at this point. My best weapon was pretending to go along, at least for a while.

He took a sip of wine. "Yes. I never had the heart to remarry. It was too painful." He looked over at me, "I always regretted that we never had a child. There are times when it's lonely living in this house. I hope that we can be friends, Bernadette. We can be mutually beneficial to one another."

Being best buddies with this psycho was the last thing I wanted, but I forced a smile. "It seems to me that I'm more beneficial to you at this point. If you can assure me of my parents and my friends' safety, I'll cooperate. I need hear my parents and friends' voices telling me they're okay."

He nodded and then passed a platter of the lamb, to me. "That can be arranged after we dine. Your loved ones are safe, even if their movement has to be restricted. They have plenty of food and there's always Netflix for entertainment."

It was awkward with the bulky gloves, but I helped myself to salad and some shrimp. "You said that you want to use my powers to save the world. I'm not sure how you're going to do that." I might as well find out more of his lunatic plans. There might be something I'd learn that could help me deal with him.

He finished swallowing and then placed his hands on the table. "Okay, let's take the climate crisis. Sea levels are rising, freshwater supplies are diminishing, and catastrophic storms threaten food production. Someone like you could help with the food easily enough, but it may also be in your power to affect the climate as well. You've heard of cloud seeding in drought-stricken areas. Why not harness your power in that manner? Have you ever changed the weather?"

I blinked a couple of times, gawking at him. Change the weather? I'd produced balls of fire in my palms. What if that energy could be used to still a hurricane or tropical storm? I'd never considered that this could be done, let alone that I'd be able to do it. But my power had grown so much in such a brief time that I couldn't rule it out.

"No. I've never tried to do that. I'm not sure I could." Lies could fly off my tongue easily in the face of Bloomstein's threats. I had to downplay whatever abilities I had to keep him off balance. He already knew I could conjure gold and killer bees; I'd just as soon keep him waiting about any of my other gifts.

He smiled and resumed eating. "That's just one of the tests we'll do. Your hands contain power as I've seen. And what is power but energy? Harnessed in the right way, I don't see how you wouldn't affect change in weather patterns."

"But fresh water and the rising sea? That's asking too much." But even I knew that if weather could be changed, it would influence the sea level rising. I might have to create a giant freezer to lower world's temperature or something.

"This is something that my physicists are more qualified to answer. They tend to the details while I'm more of a big picture guy. And you won't be alone. If we clone you, we can produce an army of people with your power. We need you to prepare the way, so there will be a world to improve upon."

I sat back and stared at him. "But this isn't all about saving the planet, is it? You said it yourself. You want to extend your life. That's the *real thing* you want, right?"

He laughed. "You get to the heart of things quickly, Bernadette. Yes, of course that's what I want. Who wouldn't? But I don't want to extend my life only to continue as a frail old man. I desire my health and mental faculties to be that of a man half my age. Your youth, your vitality can be harnessed to achieve that."

"What? You sound like some kind of rich old vampire. I think you'd suck my blood to become young." Yuck. The salad churned up into the back of my throat. There was no way his shriveled old lips were coming anywhere near my neck.

"You watch too many movies. Have you never heard of stem cells? These are cells that can, with some modification, become *any* cell in your body. For example, if your liver is degrading, infuse it with stems. Same with brain cells. Stem cells are where the magic happens, Bernadette."

"You want my *stem* cells? Where exactly are these cells in my body? My spleen or heart or..." I shuddered inwardly. "... my ovaries?"

He slapped the table and practically giggled. "Yes, that boyfriend Paul certainly underestimated you! You're close to the truth of it, Bernadette. The very best stem cells are contained in the placenta when you give birth. And that is exactly what I desire; for you to give birth."

I stood up so fast the chair toppled over. "No. Way. If you think I'm having a baby with you, you're crazy!" The shrimp I'd eaten was now close to jettisoning out of my stomach. Eew. The guy had to be almost eighty! How could he even *think* of such a thing?

"Relax. There doesn't have to be any physical contact between us. I've got a plethora of sperm cells stored, from when I was a young man." The edge left his voice when he continued. "It's for the greater good, Bernadette. The world needs men like me and women with your ability. Everyone benefits."

I picked up my chair and took a seat once more. "Okay, I take it back. I'm not just a lab rat, I'm now in the *Handmaid's Tale*! You want me to be a breeder! This just keeps getting better and better." Yuck. It still was revolting. I had to find a way out of this lunatic's house before *that* happened.

Bloomstein shook his head. "Never read the book, I'm afraid, but I did watch a few episodes on cable. It's ironic how often science follows fiction sometimes."

"If you're through with dinner, I'd like to speak to my parents and then my friends. That's the only way I will let you go through with this. But for the record, I think this is monstrous."

And definitely *not* going to happen, if I had anything to do with it.

"No dessert?" Bloomstein set his napkin on the table and rose. "We'll adjourn to the library, if you don't mind. We will place the call there." As he walked out of the room, he slipped his cell phone from his pocket.

When the door opened, the same thug who'd escorted me from the basement stood there. "Carl, would you mind placing the call for Bernadette to speak with her parents?" He continued down the hallway and entered the arched doorway where walls of books from ceiling to floor dominated. At the far end of the room was an enormous fireplace with wingback chairs on either side.

I took a seat in the closest one, trying to see out a set of windows for any hint of where we might be. Only the black shapes of mountains in the distance and forested fields showed. Carl handed me the phone, and I saw my mother and father staring from the small screen.

I had to fight the lump in my throat when I spoke. "Mom? Dad? Are you okay?"

"Bernadette! Where are you? What's going on?" Dad's eyes were wide, staring at me. Beside him, my mother swiped a tear from her cheek.

"I'm okay. I don't know where I am. But I'm more concerned about you! Have they hurt you?"

At a nod from Bloomstein, Carl snatched the phone from my hand and ended the call. I could have slapped the both of them right then and there. I'd hardly been able to say two words to my parents.

The phone was extended once more, and I saw Prudence on the screen while Darby huddled over her shoulder. Prudence's eyes flashed wide seeing my face. "Bernadette. Did Paul's uncle abduct you? Are you okay?"

Darby complained from behind her. "They've got us locked down here, Bern!"

I took a deep breath and tried to keep my voice even when I answered. "I'm okay for now. I'm doing whatever they ask so I can help you get free." An idea began to take seed in my head. "How's my dog? I hope you're able to get him outside so he can relieve himself. He likes the *park* near the water best. Make sure you take him there."

Pru's forehead wrinkled as she listened to what had to be an odd request. Faellin had been using the back parking lot of the hotel for the last few days, so what I asked had to sound weird.

Faellin barked in the background and this time tears rolled from my eyes. My poor dog. "Let me see him!"

The thug, Carl, tried to grab the phone from my hand but I turned away. "Not yet!" When I looked at the screen, Faellin's face filled it. "Who's a good boy! Manaan thinks you're a good boy! Do you miss Manaan? Manaan needs to come see you, Faellin. Soon."

This time the thug did get the phone from my grip. His eyes narrowed, and he scowled at me. "Who's Manaan? What was all that about?"

I sneered at him. "It's what I call myself, *fool!* Mama was too corny, so I use Manaan when I talk to my dog. Got a problem with that?"

At a flick of the wrist from Bloomstein, Carl stepped back. "It's just some kind of baby talk, Carl." Turning his gaze to me, he smiled. "Satisfied? They are all fine, as long as you cooperate."

My eyes welled with tears again and I let them flow freely. "I miss my parents and friends. And my poor dog doesn't know what's going on, why I'm not there. Can you do me a favor, Mr. Bloomstein? Can you let Pru and Darby take my dog for a run along the shore? I know your guards will be there, but my dog..." I covered my face with my hands and really let the waterworks flood my eyes. Part of it was an act, but part was totally genuine.

How pathetic was I that my best chance of getting out of this depended on my dog? If I'd been there, putting my hands on his head, I would have a better chance of getting my message through to him. He needed to summon Manaan. The old sea god had said that if I ever needed him, to stand at the shore and call his name. That Faellin, the dog of war I'd taken from Lugh, would somehow be able to do this was a total long shot. But at this point, I was willing to try anything.

Bloomstein leaned forward, and I had to make myself suffer the repulsion of his tap on my knee. "Bernadette, don't cry. Look, I'm a reasonable man. Some would even say a kind man, given the many charities which I fund. I can see that your dog's needs are important to you. It's a minor thing in the scheme of things. If it will ease your mind, then I'll give instructions to my men to arrange that walk in the park."

I put my hand on his and looked into his eyes. "You would?"

He nodded, "Certainly! I'd like us to be friends. I could even bring your dog here, if that would help."

Uh oh. That would totally screw up my plan, as harebrained as it was. "That's okay. It might be harder on me seeing him here. Plus, he's a comfort to Prudence." I forced a wan smile, "He really likes Hunter's Point Park, where he can run. It's not that far from the hotel."

"Of course. I'll see that it happens." He sat back, steepling his fingers as he watched me. "Are you more assured now that I'll treat you and your family fairly?"

"Yeah, I guess." I closed my eyes for a moment and then slumped lower. "I am bagged. After the day I had, I need some sleep." The truth of the matter was that I was totally sick of seeing his mottled old skin and the yellowed teeth. I needed to be alone to think.

He rose and then gave a slight nod to Carl. These guys were like trained lapdogs responding immediately and escorting me across the room. Before I went through the doorway, Bloomstein called out to me.

"Sleep well, Bernadette. Tomorrow is a big day."

I nodded and then went out of the room. However, sleep was the last thing on my mind. I had to get out of this crazy situation.

Fifteen

My 'bedroom', if you could call it that, was more like a room in an ICU unit with a stiff hospital bed and little else. A window opening onto another room, where one of the female medical staff sat overlooking my bed, was an added intrusion. They weren't leaving me unguarded for one minute, and they still had my hands in the stupid isolation gloves.

When I climbed into the bed, the lights dimmed a bit but I still felt like a tropical fish in a fishbowl. How was I going to get out of this mess I was in and not put my family in any further danger? Try as I might to think of any skill that I possessed, nothing would work without dire consequences.

Even if I shape shifted into a rat and managed to escape, they still had my parents and Darby and Pru held hostage. Transitioning back to Otherworld to enlist the help of Lugh and Angus would leave my loved ones vulnerable until I could return.

One option might be to try to transition to my parents' home. I could take out the thugs guarding Mom and Dad, and at least they'd be safe. But what about Darby and Pru? Even Faellin? Could I also get there before Bloomstein realized what I'd done? Lugh had told me that it wasn't possible to transition across Otherworld. The only way that trick worked was when you wanted to transition *out* of Otherworld. Would that restriction apply here?

Wait. A. Damn. Minute!

I'm a Celestial, not just a god like Lugh! I had greater powers! This might work!

There was only one way to find out. I rolled over and sneaked a peak at the nurse outside. Her focus seemed to be on the space directly in front of her, like she was reading a book or a tablet. But trying to escape with teleportation was best done later, when she might nod off and the guards attending Mom and Dad would be less alert. That meant another few hours, pretending to sleep.

There was nothing to do but wait. I let myself think of Lugh. Had he got to the northern part of his kingdom to quell the dissent brewing there? Did he even *care* that I'd left his world? Angus and Flidais were probably still angry with me over my meddling in their relationship. As irritating as it had been living with Lugh's defensive machismo, it sure beat being abducted first by a mafia thug and then a rich psychopath.

To think, all of this had started when I'd written that song and sang it at the Moon Pond in Ireland.

My eyes flashed open. Singing! What an idiot I was. It was always a powerful ability! I started humming and then broke out singing the song that had put Antonio and his guys to sleep.

After a few moments the door to my room opened and the nurse, a forty-something-year-old black chick, peered at me.

"What are you doing?"

I managed a sheepish smile. "It's how I fall asleep. I sing for a while and then I drift off. I didn't realize it would bother you."

Her forehead tightened while she shook her head. "Weird. But I guess that's why you're here, right? Knock yourself out." She closed the door and went back to her station.

I only hoped that she was the only nurse till morning. Continuing my song, I kept peeking out at her. After a few choruses of the Irish Lullaby that had worked on Morc's brother, I saw her head nod forward before she caught herself, stretching her neck to fight the drowsiness. The glass petition probably weakened the power of my singing, so I continued until her head dropped and stayed there.

Okay. This was it. I pictured my parents' home with as much detail as I could, narrowing my focus on my bedroom. There was a good chance that no one would be in it, so my arrival would go unnoticed until it was too late. Transitioning took much longer than it had when I left Otherworld. Was the same weird magnetic field that Lugh had talked about also happening here? But then I remembered how he'd gone to that island in northern Canada to fight Morc and the brothers. It had worked for Lugh, so it had to work for me.

The bed seemed to shake under me and then a stream of lights arced in my mind's eye. My stomach rolled at the strange sensation, but I kept my head zeroed in on the bedroom I'd had growing up.

There was a sensation of falling which ended abruptly. When I opened my eyes, I saw the familiar streetlight shining in through my bedroom window. Wow! My face turned to the side, taking in the furniture and the closed door. I'd done it!

The first thing I did was grab a penknife from the desk.

Mom had left pretty well everything the way it had been when I'd lived there, so it wasn't hard to find. I worked at the gloves that Bloomstein had put on me. They had to go, if I was going to be successful.

After a few minutes I held my hands up, flexing my fingers in the light from the window. With these hands, I could tackle whatever Bloomstein's thugs would throw at me. Opening my bedroom door a crack, I peeked out. The hallway outside was empty and the door to my parent's room was open a few inches. Tiptoeing, I crossed the hall to see if they were there. My eyes narrowed seeing the empty bed.

They had been downstairs on the sofa when the calls from Bloomstein's goons had come in. They must still be there, which meant that so was the big blond brute. But it would be a mistake to think he was alone.

I crept down the stairs, wincing when my foot hit one which let out a loud squeak. Shit! I should have remembered that one from sneaking in late at night after being out after curfew. Listening hard, the only sound was my father snoring. That was good.

Continuing on, I peered across the hall into the kitchen where only the light from the stove vent hood broke the darkness. No strange person lurking there. With a slight sense of relief, I stepped across the floor and inched forward to see into the living room. My gut tightened seeing my parents asleep on the sofa with Dad's head on one armrest and Mom's on the opposite one.

In the wingback chair across from them was the blond bruiser. His head tipped back, but there was still a gun lying in his limp hand.

If he woke, it would be the end of not only me but also my parents. I had to somehow get that gun away from him and at the same time disable him from jumping up and attacking us. My mind went back to when Aine had used a vine to trap me when I tried to leave Flidais's home. I wished that my sister Flidais had taught me how she'd done that.

The only vine type plant in my parents' home was the ivy that Mom babied in the front window. It would break with the first bit of resistance. Nope, that kind of magic wasn't in my repertoire, not yet.

I rubbed my fingers together, and a hypodermic needle appeared in my palm. Creeping softly, I got closer to the goon. Standing nearly on top of him, my left hand shot out to grab the gun, while my other hand stabbed his neck with the needle, pushing the plunger to inject the same drug they'd used on me.

His eyes popped opened, and he fumbled for the gun, but it was in my hand pointed at his face.

"Don't move or I swear I'll shoot you!" It surprised me how steady my voice and hand were! You'd think I actually had a clue what I was doing.

"Bernadette?"

I didn't dare turn from watching the thug to answer my mother. Instead, I barked out an order. "Wake Dad up. Are there any other guys guarding you?"

"Lanny! Wake up! Hurry!"

"Mom? Who else is here?"

It was my father who answered. "No one! Bernadette! How'd you--"

"Later, Dad. Get your coats." I watched the thug's eyes blink a few times before his head tipped to the side. Whatever that drug was, it worked super-fast!

I turned to my parents. "Take this gun! Get in the car and drive far away from here. Don't stop until you get really far away!"

"But what about you? You've got to come with us!"

I shook my head. "No, Mom. I can't. I've got to get to Prudence and Darby to help them!"

Dad took the gun from me, holding it with two fingers like it was filth. "We'll drive you." He took a deep breath.

"Never mind. You do whatever it is you do. You'll be faster than my old jalopy. Just be careful!"

Mom hugged me. "Oh, my God. Be careful, Bernadette! Call us when you can." Dad had to pull her away, so he could plant a kiss on my forehead.

I watched them hurry from the room and then the door shut. A few moments later, the car's engine rumbled to life.

Just one last thing and I'd be out of there. I searched the thug's pocket and found the cell phone. I had no idea how long the drug would keep him out, considering his size, so best to delay any calls to Bloomstein.

When I had it in the pocket of my shirt, I closed my eyes picturing the hotel room where my friends were being held captive. Again, it took a long time. Too long.

At the snort of the thug in the chair, I turned. But I was too late. He was out of it and barreling towards me.

Sixteen

Before he had a chance to grab me, I dodged to the side. He stumbled into the coffee table and crashed onto the floor. The drug was still having some effect, even if it had worn off way too soon. Quick as I could, I thought of what else could keep this lout down. My hand rose and in my fist was a taser. I blasted his butt, watching him jerk up before flopping into a limp heap.

Much as I wanted to resume my attempt to transition to the hotel, I had to know if the creep was alive. I stepped by the splintered coffee table and bent to check for a pulse in his neck. Yes. He was alive, and from the look of him, that shock of electricity would keep him down for a while.

Again, I stepped away and closed my eyes to begin the process to get to the hotel. I could practically smell Darby's perfume and hear Prudence's soft slumbering snore.

Faellin's slobbery kisses on my hand along with his big brown eyes was my final thought before the familiar tingling in my body morphed into a vibration. The pinpricks of light flashed in my head and my stomach rolled.

I felt myself fall and immediately crouched lower for impact. I opened my eyes when I felt Faellin's wet nose on my ankle. Scratching behind his ear, I whispered. "It's okay, boy."

Darby and Prudence were asleep in the two queen beds, but there was no sign of any guard hanging around. That could only mean that this hotel room was now a prison cell. Locked and guarded from the outside.

Tiptoeing across the room, I reached Prudence first. "Pru! Wake up." When her eyes opened, she blinked a few times before grabbing my arm.

"Bernadette! How—"

I held my hand to her lips, shushing her. "Never mind. We need to leave this place, fast." I reached over and shook Darby's foot. "Wake up, Darby!"

She kicked at my hand, but my grip tightened around her ankle. "It's Bernadette! C'mon. We have to leave." Darby rolled over and her eyes went wide seeing me.

"What? How'd—"

"We can't leave, Bern! The door is locked and we're nine stories up in the air." Prudence threw the comforter covers back and stood up. Her eyes narrowed, "Wait. I know how you did this."

I nodded. "Yeah. The same way I went to Otherworld with Lugh and then back here to Earth. I'm afraid that there's no other way out of this mess. We don't have much time before Bloomstein realizes I'm gone."

Darby sat forward. "Hold on. You mean for us to leave like... I don't even know what to call it—whatever it is you do to get places. We can't possibly—"

"We *have* to, Darb! Either that or stay here and face the consequences. And believe me, they will get even nastier when they know I've escaped." I grabbed her hand and pulled her to her feet. "It's not scarier than staying here, trust me!"

Prudence glanced down at her body. "I'm not dressed." She finally took my hospital garb in. "Neither are you from the looks of it. What's that thing in your hand?"

I tossed it on the bed. "A taser. I had to save my mom and dad before I came here." Grabbing her hand as well, I led them over to where Faellin now sat up, wagging his tail. "Yap!"

"See? He knows what we're going to do! C'mon ladies. We gotta hold on to each other when I do this."

But Darby wasn't convinced. "Where can we go? We can't stay in the city! There's Antonio and now this rich psycho looking for us, here. Where will we be safe? They're never going to stop looking, Bernadette. Maybe we should go to the police."

All of what Darby said was true, except the part about going to the police. I gripped her hand harder. "Look we'll worry about how we're going to deal with those crooks later. Right now, the important thing is to get out of here before Bloomstein's guys came barging in!"

I looked at Pru and Darby. "Close your eyes. You might see flashing lights and feel a little nausea when this happens. It's normal." Normal? Nothing was normal anymore. Nothing had been normal since I'd gone to that Moon Pond and sang my song. And then it hit me. We didn't have to stay in New York. Hell! We didn't even need to stay in this country!

The Moon Pond in Ireland. It would give us some breathing space until I could get my family out to join us. I closed my eyes thinking of that night in Ireland, singing my song that awakened Lugh. I could feel the cool mist of the waterfall on my skin... the smell of the cedar in the forest.

Faellin growled and my eyes flew open. He sprang up, racing to the door. At his high-pitched yelp of pain, I spun around. My heart was in my throat seeing the three guys standing near the entrance to the room.

But worse was seeing Faellin lying next to the wall! Oh, my god! They'd killed Faellin? I rushed over to his side.

"Faellin!" I felt his breath on my hand and sighed with relief. At least he was alive. But why had they hurt him? Glaring at the three guys, "What did you do to him?"

The smallest one had to be six feet tall. Instead of the way I'd see Bloomstein's goons dress in their business suits like they were actually legitimate, these guys wore black helmets and bulletproof vests. The police?

Prudence stood next to me now. "Is Faellin…"

"Not dead, thank god, but he's out cold." I stood up and got right in the closest one's face. "Who the hell are you? You don't work for Bloomstein, that's for sure." They had that manner about them, like all cops I'd had any experience with; kind of authoritarian types, taking control. It wasn't helping that they hadn't answered my question.

Darby came over, standing next to us. "You're here to save us, right? You arrested those guys who kidnapped us? What are you, FBI?"

Finally, the one in charge, a black guy who looked like a young Samuel Jackson spoke. "We're here to escort you ladies to safety. Grab your coats if you have any. Which one of you is Bernadette Adelson?"

I glared at him. "I'm Bernadette. If you guys are cops, let me see your badges. I've had enough of goons barging in on us, and then abducting me and my friends. I'm not going anywhere until I see some I.D."

Excruciating pain ripped through my body! I shook, unable to move as it continued for what seemed like hours. And then everything went black.

Seventeen

B ernadette? C'mon honey, wake up." A soft feminine voice drifted in the air beside me. I felt warmth and something rubbing my arm.

Oh God. My head felt like a jackhammer pounded my forehead, splitting my head in two. At another voice, this time Darby's, my eyes fluttered and then opened. Prudence swiped away a tear as she hovered above me, while Darby's face was tight with worry lines. When I tried to sit up, something kept me locked down tight. I couldn't even wiggle my fingers. Hell, I could hardly *feel* them.

"What... what happened?" It was hard to get the words past my tongue that felt like a ball of cotton. The ceiling above me glared with bright lights. Squinting, I saw that I was lying on a bed of stainless steel. And then it started to come back to me...

"Where's Faellin? Is he all right?"

Darby swore under her breath. "Those bastards just left him laying there. They crammed the three of us into a black SUV and drove us here, with hoods over our heads. I don't know who those guys are, but they aren't regular cops, that's for sure."

Prudence added, "They *tased* you, Bern. You blacked out and then they scooped you up like a rag doll. I'm pretty sure they aren't with Bloomstein. His guys weren't military like the ones who brought us here. I don't know who they are. Russians, maybe."

Footsteps from across the room caught my attention and two guys in black suits edged Prudence and Darby to the side. It was one face in particular I focused on. Where had I seen him? When he spoke it hit me in an instant. And the fact that he was built like a linebacker reinforced it. He was one of Bloomstein's orderlies — one of the guys that escorted me to dinner with the old geezer.

"I see you recognize me, Bernadette. Yes, I was working undercover at Bloomstein's. He's been conducting research into cryogenics and cloning, which the government was keeping an eye on. Of course, human cloning is illegal, but—"

"But you set all that aside when he brought in a specimen like me. That's it. All your surveillance ended when you found me there." It was as clear as anything in his mind. He didn't even look surprised that I'd gleaned this.

The other guy, a swarthy Latino with a receding hairline, chuckled. "You caught us all off guard when you just disappeared from the lab. And then appeared immediately somewhere else to free your parents. It was lucky for us we were able to apprehend you before you vanished again! How'd you do that, anyway?"

Ignoring the Latino guy, I turned to the other one. "Carl. That's your name, right? Why are you keeping my friends? You've got me secured here. Let them go. They've got nothing to do with this. At least let them go look after my dog."

His face screwed up into a sneer. "What's with you and that dog? He'll be fine. The animal control people were dispatched to get him."

The Latino guy coughed. "Uh,... no, Carl. They called me to let me know the animal escaped. They fired tranquilizers, and he took a few hits but that damned mutt just kept going."

Carl shook his head. "No matter. They'll get him. It's no concern to us." He looked down at me silently for a few moments. "As for your friends, I'm afraid they must remain here with you. We can't take a chance that Bloomstein won't find them. Your parents' cell phones led our agents to their location. They'll be under our protection."

"We're not like Bloomstein or that other low-life mafia guy, Antonio. You're a U.S. citizen and we'll treat you well. But..."

"But, you want to know how I do this." I scowled at the Latino guy. "What makes you so much better than Bloomstein or Antonio? You all have your own agenda."

Carl answered me. "Except our agenda involves national security. That's hardly a petty matter, Bernadette. It would be wonderful if you'd cooperate and let us determine how you can do the things you do, like creating things out of nothing, vanishing only to appear in other places. But, even if you won't willingly let us investigate, we can't risk any of our enemies getting their hands on you."

My eyes narrowed, and I tried to sit up. Shit! "Aren't you afraid I might just pull another disappearing act? Do you think these heavy straps can stop me?"

"No. But I don't think you'll want to leave without your friends." The Latino guy looked across the room and then Darby let out a yell.

"No wait! We're not leaving Bernadette! I demand to see a lawyer. Bernadette's father!"

Pru's voice followed. "Get you grimy hands off me! I'll knock you into tomorrow!"

Their cries and protests finished when a loud bang, like a door closing, resounded in the air. Movement to the side, showed a portly woman in a white uniform stepping closer, She held a hypodermic needle up and tapped the tube to get any air bubbles out.

Carl's head tipped to the side. "I know this looks like the tactics that Bloomstein used but until we can be assured you will remain here and cooperate, we must sedate you. It's our educated guess that for you to do any of your tricks, you need a clear head."

"Tricks? That's what you guys call what I do?"

Carl just shrugged, and the other guy concurred as the nurse pricked my shoulder with the needle. "We hope that you'll remember that you're a U.S. citizen. You have a patriotic duty to help your country, Bernadette."

The last of his words sounded like they were coming from an echo chamber. My eyes fluttered closed, and that was the last I saw of the agents. Damn, I was getting sick of always being drugged.

Eighteen

The drone of an electronic beep penetrated my head, but I kept my eyes shut. I listened hard for any sound of human activity in the room where they had me confined. So far it was just the machine and me.

A quick peek, scanning the room, confirmed it. But the machine making the noise was about six feet away, showing three fluctuating lines across the small screen. It was some kind of monitor they'd hooked me up to.

The click of a door handle was followed by brisk footsteps. "Ah, Bernadette! You're finally awake." It was Carl…I'm seeing way too much of this guy. He was smiling, but it never reached the stony glint in his eyes.

Fine by me. If they thought that I was going to jump through their hoops willingly, they had another think coming. "Where are my friends?"

Carl stared silently at me before his fingers tapped the inside crook of my arm.

"Oow!" I lifted my head as much as I could to see how he'd managed to shoot an arrow of pain up my arm. Shit! They had my arm hooked up to an intravenous tube! The sadistic bastard had tapped the needle that was lodged in my vein.

God, I was so sick of this shit! My eyes squeezed shut, along with my teeth clamping tight together. But it wasn't only my face that I willingly closed off. Goosebumps rose all over my body as my skin contracted. I felt a slight pop. I glanced down and my eyes widened seeing the intravenous needle lying on the mattress, no longer in my arm.

"Hey! Nurse, come help me!" Carl reached for the needle but his hand froze about two inches away from it.

And I definitely meant 'froze'. My eyes narrowed as I projected freezing cold at him. His fingers became white with bluish fingernails. I was totally *done* with being kidnapped, with my family and friends threatened and being treated like a pincushion!

"Stop!" Carl's wrist showed that the frostbite was travelling up his arm. He tried pulling back, but my mind wasn't letting him move.

Now who was scared and hurt? I was still tied into this bed, but I could lay a hurting on one of them at least.

Movement at my other side caught my attention. The nurse he'd summoned stood next to the bed, holding the needle in her hand. She jabbed it, but instead of stabbing into my skin, it flew across the room as if she'd tried to pierce steel.

The rage inside me grew wilder still. With another effort of will, I focused on the straps keeping me secured to this bed, and the bindings covering my fingers. My body shook as I imagined all of these trappings flying off and wrapping tight over the goons on either side of me.

Carl's yells and the nurse's high-pitched cry was a muted

background as I channeled all my energy into freeing myself. Time slowed to a crawl as I mentally struggled to control the two of them and loosen the straps. All at once, my nylon bindings flew up and off.

I pushed myself higher, watching Carl become snared in the strap. And just like what Aine had done to me, the strap became longer, wrapping around and around his body, securing his arms tight to his torso. At the yelp out of the nurse, I saw that the same process was happening to her.

"Yes! I did it." A grin lifted my face, and I gave a fist bump to the universe! I had learned to do the same thing Aine had done, and I'd done it all by myself! Never again was I going to get injected with drugs and tied up. It was time to start hitting back.

"Please. Make it stop. I... can't breathe." Carl's lips were turning a purplish shade, so I knew he was telling the truth.

With just a thought, I eased the band off both him and the nurse. They could breathe, but there was no way either of them were going anywhere soon. "I asked you a question, Carl. Where are my friends? They better be okay or I'm afraid *you* won't be."

"They're in another part of the building. They're fine, but they can't leave. I can take you to them. Just, please stop this pressure." Some color had returned to his lips, even though his eyes were wide with terror.

"You'll have to do better than that. You see, I'm tired of being everyone's guinea pig. You will summon whoever is in charge of this operation. That person will not only escort my friends here, but they'll join us when we escape." I smiled at him. "That will be my little insurance policy. You see... two can play that game."

Carl's eyes went wider still. "I can't! General Cormant isn't even at this facility. He's in Washington, waiting for our report. I can request that your friends be brought here, but that's it. They'll never allow you to leave though."

I tightened the straps over his chest and watched him

gasp, struggling to breathe. What Carl wasn't aware of was the fact that I'd read his thoughts, which totally contradicted his words. This General Cormant was here in the compound, not Washington. "Are you sure he isn't around? It would be a shame if your lungs collapsed trying to protect some bureaucratic psycho."

"He's here!"

I jerked a little, hearing the nurse who was also having the literal screws tighten around her chest.

I turned to her. I knew Carl was lying. "What's your name?"

"J... Ju... Judy! I'm a doctor. A psychiatrist who specializes in parapsychology. Let me go and I'll help you. I never wanted to be part of this, but they forced me." Her fingers tore at the straps trying to loosen them.

I watched her closely, going past the superficial outside appearance of dark terror filled eyes. Her thoughts centered on having to leave a toddler with a woman who resembled Judy so much that I knew it was her mother. She'd spent many years in school on a military scholarship that she was still trying to repay with service. Her main objective in this was getting home to her family. In some ways she was as much a prisoner as me; trapped in financial binds.

"Okay, Judy. I will trust you. I'll loosen your binds, and you will summon the guards to bring my friends here. After that, you'll insist that General Cormant meet with me. This is his project, so he is ultimately responsible." I sat up and walked over to where she was, ignoring Carl. When I loosened Judy's binds, I also gave Carl some breathing room. I wasn't a total jerk, after all. But I'd definitely had enough of playing by their rules.

Judy pulled a cell phone from her pocket and spoke into it. "This is Dr. Palmer. We need you to bring the subject's friends to the lab." There was silence during which she rolled her eyes before practically barking an order. "I don't care what the original directive was. This is new based on a developing situation."

Just as I was about to thank Judy, the lights in the room went out. For a moment I froze. Shit! There were probably cameras in the room so that whatever happened could not only be seen but recorded. How had I not foreseen that possibility? Now they had the upper hand once again.

I rubbed my fingers together, and a small flame arced above them. In the low light I could see Judy staring at me, shaking her head. "I didn't do this, Bernadette. For what it's worth, I'd leave if I were you. I mean *right now*! They're never going to let you go."

"Dr. Palmer! You'll stop encouraging her, if you know what's good for you. We've treated her fair and—"

"Listen!" I held my hand up to silence him. There was a very low hiss and an odor in the air.

Even before Judy spoke, I knew what was their next trick. They couldn't drug me with a needle, so they were going to gas me to put me under.

Oh shit.

Nineteen

I had to get out of there fast before the drug seeping into the room took hold. I closed my eyes and pictured Hunter's Point Park. Not only was the park next to the water so that I could summon Manaan to help me, but there was a strong possibility that Faellin would be there. I'd have to trust that these government agents wouldn't actually hurt my friends... not for a while at least.

The smell of the gas was getting stronger and I really put my mind to work imagining the park in all its details. The flame on my fingertips extinguished, and I felt that tingling begin there, rolling up and into my core. My stomach rolled when the pinpricks of light once more flooded my head.

I landed on my side, knocking the wind out of me. Opening my eyes, the green grass and smell of flowers hit me. Perfect! It was the park! I recognized the boardwalk close to the water's edge, the line of trees and the backdrop of tall buildings. It was early in the day, judging by the glow of the sun behind a bank of grey clouds. Pushing myself up, I scanned the park for signs of people who might have witnessed my sudden appearance. There were already too many people who had seen my magical abilities. That's what had started all the trouble I was in.

Thankfully, there was only a group of preschoolers being herded by two teachers on an outing. I noticed a blur from the corner of my eye. A furry blur of wolfhound descended on me and I heard the wonderful, joyful 'Yap!'

Faellin! He knocked me back on my butt when he jumped up, putting his paws on my shoulders. "Good boy!" It was hard to get the words out with all the dog kisses his slobbery mouth laid on my face. I rubbed my hands over his head, scratching behind his ears and trying to see what was going on inside his head. I could feel his irritation when the animal control had cornered him and shot four tranquilizers into his side. But he'd managed to dart by them and the snare they tried to capture him with. Thankfully, he was okay, and he hadn't hurt anyone.

When he sprang up and barked, heading for the water's edge I trailed after him. I watched an eddy appear in the smooth surface of the river and I did a double take. Oh, my god! I rubbed Faellin's head while tears welled in my eyes. "Good boy! You did it! You knew that I wanted you to summon Manaan!"

Faellin let out a loud bark before nuzzling his mouth into my hand. He was as happy to see Manaan as I was.

The ship rose higher in the water as it approached the shore. A glance around me showed people going about their business, oblivious to the fact that an ancient sea god was emerging in a mystical craft. I remembered the first time Manaan had appeared in Ireland. At that time, I hadn't been able to see the ship either. The sight of it now brought a fresh set of tears.

I wasn't alone in my battle with all these thugs who wanted to cash in on my power. And for Homeland Security (or whatever the hell branch of the government Carl and the General were connected to) was just another power grab. Mobsters or Generals, it was no difference. All of them wanted to use me for their own ends.

Faellin let out another 'Yap!' and his tail swung like mad when the craft nudged the rocky shoreline. A door slid open and a gang plank extended over the water and rocks, ending at my feet. Manaan stepped forward, filling the door frame and beckoning to me.

"Bernadette! You're here! I was sorely worried when your hound summoned me. I feared the worst. Come aboard."

I raced down the ramp and stepped into his ship. Throwing my arms around his neck, I let the dam holding my tears break.

All of it hit me at once. My mother's treachery and death, so shortly after meeting her for the first time, leaving Otherworld—and Lugh not giving much of a damn, my sister, Angus, my parents... In just the last few weeks so much had happened in my life that it just... no, *finally* overwhelmed me. The images of all that had happened since I took that walk to the 'Moon Pond' rolled over me like a giant wave, drowning me.

I cried like a three-year-old with a playground boo-boo.

Manaan held me in his arms in a firm clasp, rubbing my back as the tears and sobs poured out of me. He didn't tell me 'shhh', he didn't say 'there, there'... No, he just held onto to me; keeping me from falling away into the depths of hopelessness. He held onto me as my soul rent in two, and as I knitted it back together.

When I was done; when there were no more tears or sobs left in my heart, I simply held him. We stood in the hatch of his magical craft as it bobbed up and down in the water while my breathing returned to normal.

I kept my cheek smushed against his chest as his hand caressed the back of my head. "Thanks," I said. "I *really* needed that."

"Ahhh child…" he said, his voice holding the tenor of the oceans. "Aye, and it's been a labor for ye these days…"

I shuddered in agreement. "I don't know if I'm cut out for this, Manaan…I mean—this whole 'Celestial' thing… it's been more of a curse than blessing."

"With great power comes great responsibility, lass." He put his hands on my shoulders and stepped back. He looked me up and down. "You're such a slip of a girl, Bernadette. The truth of your nature is still so new to you."

I felt my chin doing that pre-bawl-out-loud tremble again as I stared back at him.

He gave me a brisk shake. "No more of that, lassie. You've cried enough. You're a powerful creature, but like a newborn. You'll find your way in all this."

"I… I'm not so sure…"

"Bernadette!" He gave me another shake. "It doesn't *matter* what you may or may not be 'sure' about! It's what it is! You're a Celestial! And you're a strong, good-hearted, intelligent woman! You've come brilliantly far in mastering your abilities in such a scant time!" He gave me a final shake that was more like a hug. "And you're not alone."

His eyes were soft with concern. His white hair floated in the air next to his face, the way I'd seen it the first time I'd met him. I burst out with the first thing on my mind.

"I've really made a mess of things, Manaan! People, *bad people*, have found out about my powers and they're trying to get me to work for them. They're using my family and friends as hostages to get me to do what they want. And they've got guns! I couldn't even sic Faellin on them because they'd *shoot* him!"

His lips were a straight line while his eyes had darkened hearing me blubber. "This cannot be allowed to happen to you… not to a Celestial! Those buffoons! Why did you not employ some of the things you learned? Shape shift? Or conjure up your *own* weapon?" He shook his head. "My apologies, Lady Bernadette; this is new to you. How could you know how to fight back?"

"Can you help me? Or get Lugh and Angus to help me? I thought of getting a weapon, but I'm no gun expert. I'd probably screw that up too! I wish Flidais had taught me more when I was with her. Maybe she'd come to help as well?"

He pulled me into his arms when a fresh set of tears wracked my shoulders. "Of course I'll help you. I can send a couple of my crew with you now. There'll be more once I put out the call. Or better yet, stay here with me until these thugs can be dealt with."

"I can't. My friends, Darby and Prudence, are being held in some government facility. I'm hoping Faellin can track it down so that I can try to free them. If I disappear, they may do something terrible to Darby and Pru. And they know where my parents are too." There was no way I'd ever let anything happen to any of them.

Manaan's head dropped, and he looked at me from under his bushy eyebrows. "You are forgetting your gifts, Bernadette. As for Faellin…" He reached down and rubbed the dog's head. "… you can create a coat of armor to protect him from these guns. I suggest you do that. You will then have a dog of war at your side. He hates being left out of this. This is who he is, after all."

"Yes!" I pictured a set of bullet proof body armor that would fit the large wolfhound. At the sudden weight in my hands, I opened my eyes to behold an enormous doggy coat. Except this was constructed of black Kevlar like riot cops wore, with ceramic plates sewn in as well. I had read that they were called 'shock plates' or something. It would cover him from his head to his tail.

Manaan laughed as I tugged the coat over Faellin's body.

All the while the dog looked at me with big sad eyes, trying to step away but being coerced into wearing the heavy garment.

"Faellin! If this is good enough for New York's finest, it's good enough for you! Hold still." I pressed the Velcro fastener at his neck and stood up. That was one problem dealt with.

Turning back to Manaan, "You'll get Lugh? And Angus and Flidais?" But then I remembered that Lugh was off in the north fighting his own battles. Maybe he couldn't help me.

Manaan picked up my thoughts and nodded. "Yes, Lugh is fighting his own battles, Bernadette. That is why you must rely on yourself and my two guards in this matter." He clasped my shoulders. "Remember who you are, Bernadette. Or as they say here, 'Don't let the bastards grind you down.'"

"I will. But where are your guys? Will they come with me now?"

"No. That would not be wise. They will remain hidden, watching over you until needed." He gave a sharp nod of his head. "Too many humans have seen beings from Otherworld for my liking; they'll remain unseen until necessary."

"How will I know it's them? Will they look like the men you sent to my parents?"

He chuckled. "You'll know them when they appear, believe me. They'll be wearing my sigil— a series of waves on their chests."

"Okay." I hugged him one last time. "I'd better get back to my friends. Any more words of advice before I leave?"

He took my hand and turned it over so that my palm faced him. "Trust yourself, Bernadette. These hands don't just create things, they're weapons too. I wouldn't want to be the man who tried to hurt you. There is power here that you need to harness. Just as you can commandeer elements in the earth and air to come forth and create, so too can these elements be pushed out from you. Your opponents may have guns and bullets, but you can throw *thunderbolts* with these hands."

I held my hands up and blinked looking at them. Thunderbolts. Yes, thanks to losing my temper, I'd managed to escape the government thugs. It was well past the time to fight back, and fight back hard. Squatting down, I placed my hands on Faellin's head, looking into his big brown eyes.

"We need to find Pru and Darby, Faellin. You need to track the scent of those guys from last night. And when we find the place where they're keeping them, you will join me in the battle. No more holding back for you either, boy!"

He stood up and nuzzled my cheek. I didn't need to discern what was going on inside the great hound's head. It was apparent from his wagging tail and his whines urging us to get going.

There was just one other thing I needed to do before we left the safety of Manaan's ship. I held my hands up picturing a leather jacket, a dark hoodie and black jeans. There was no way I was wearing surgical scrubs any longer. I slipped the new clothes on and turned to face Manaan. "All set."

He led the way to the hatch of his ship. "Don't worry about your parents, Bernadette. It won't take long for me to dispatch the same team who guarded them once before." As I slipped by him, he grasped my arm, stopping me. "In a brief time you've acquired many enemies, all with plans to exploit you. I must ask Bernadette, is this how you wish to live your life?"

He'd hit on something that had been niggling in the back of my mind since the encounter with Paul's uncle, Antonio. There would always be ruthless people trying to control and use my gifts. I looked into his eyes and shook my head. "No. I honestly thought I could do some good in my world; try to help people less fortunate." I snorted. "The one psychopath who kidnapped me wanted me to solve the climate change crises. I actually think he may have been onto something with that. Now my government is afraid I'll be used by Russia or China or something."

Manaan's head tipped to the side, skewering me with the intensity of his gaze. "What exactly do *you* want Bernadette? You must decide what is important to you. Once you do, your path will become clear."

I shrugged. "Right now, I'm focusing on freeing Pru and Darby. That's all I can think about for now. After... well..."

Manaan smiled. "I understand. Save your friends. That's the most important thing to you. I will return and when I do, I will not be alone." He gave me a kiss on the forehead before I turned to walk off the ship with Faellin.

Scouting out the park for any signs of the government or Bloomstein's guys, I heard the door shut and the churn of water as Manaan's ship left. The coast was still clear, aside from a young woman walking her Sheepdog along the pathway. Her eyes were round as marbles as she stared at Faellin and me. From her perspective, she'd only seen us walk above the water and then step onto the shoreline.

I fluttered my fingers at her as I walked by. There was no time for any smart ass remark or explanation. "C'mon Faellin. Lead the way to Prudence and Darby."

Faellin sniffed the air and then took off across the park, heading for the street. I held on to the leash I'd created for him and did my best to keep up. I toyed with the idea of shifting into a wolfhound again to make things faster but with the increased traffic in the area, it would create more problems.

We jogged through Queens, passing through residential neighborhoods and commercial districts lined with shops and boutiques. Eventually the shops and homes gave way to a section filled with warehouses and distribution centers. I called for Faellin to stop. Not only did I need to catch my breath, but I wanted to double check with the dog that he was leading me to my friends. Next to one of the warehouses was a park bench near a bus stop. I sat on it, and Faellin sat at my feet.

Again, my hands roamed over the great hound's head, trying to discern what was going on there. Immediately, I sensed the image of Prudence in his head. He knew what he was doing! Not surprising that it would be Pru who'd registered in his head. Darby never went too close to Faellin because of her allergies, but Pru was always affectionate to him.

"Faellin, what would I do without you?" I leaned over and planted a kiss on the top of his head. "We'll find them." About five minutes later, with my wind back, I stood up. "Let's go, boy!"

It wasn't long before Faellin leaped and strained against his leash in excitement. It could only mean we were close, I looked around. Now I was totally confused standing at an intersection. One road led down past more warehouses and businesses, while in the other direction was a vast park dotted with softball diamonds. Again, I had to trust to Faellin's nose that he knew the way to go. When he led the way to the park, I hoped that this wasn't just because he needed a bio break.

But he practically ran through it, heading to another road that ran alongside the ocean. We travelled about half a mile before he turned. From where I stood, it looked like a construction site with heavy earthmoving equipment. But Faellin's reaction bordered on being frantic, tugging at the leash. When we'd gone past the gigantic machines, I could see why.

Tucked in behind some trees and a crane was a cement block building. You could have easily missed it if you weren't looking. It was the perfect spot for a secret government building, hiding in plain sight.

It looked like they abandoned it with no cars or people around. But Faellin's bouncing around told me it was anything but deserted. The entire building was windowless, and the front entrance was a steel door. The windows were covered with security bars and the large door at the front looked like the entrance to a fortress. Now the problem was getting inside and then finding my friends.

At the sound of a vehicle turning into the driveway, I darted behind a bulldozer, holding Faellin at my side as I peeped to see. Sure enough, it was a black SUV with tinted windows that drove past. It stopped at the end of the building, in front of a blank wall. As I watched, the wall silently slid over to the side, revealing a ramp heading underground. The SUV entered, and again, the wall slid shut behind it. That was it. If Faellin and I could sneak in that way, we might have a chance of finding Darby and Pru.

But those agents would be expecting that I'd return for my friends. What they wouldn't be expecting would be two Irish wolfhounds roaming the building. They had no idea that I could shape shift. That could be the advantage I'd been looking for.

I studied the secret entranceway. I couldn't see anything but the solid wall. Not a window, nor doorway. But... off to one side was a small silver box with a tiny, red light blinking. From my time as a prisoner, I recognized it as an electronic sensor. I bet that it controlled the doorway I just watched. If I could mentally control it, I could get in.

I darted over, held my hand over the box and pushing my energy out from my fingertips, I imagined a magnet. Magnets could damage credit cards, so why not a reader?

Nothing happened though. I looked down at Faellin, who sprung up and raced to the door. I could hardly believe my eyes when the door rumbled and then started to open. As I hurried to get inside, I noticed an electronic laser beam beside the door. Faellin had tripped it when I'd disabled the reader. Not only was his sense of smell better than mine, he had a better sense of electronics!

I snickered. "Tech support from a dog! What a Celestial,

Bernadette!" I went over and petted Faellin. "Good boy! Now stay with me." I closed my eyes and pictured a wolfhound in my mind. It wasn't hard with Faellin at my side. The familiar stretching and vibration of every cell in my body began. I smelled the car exhaust and engine oil along with gasoline. When my eyes opened, I saw Faellin's nose sniffing at my ear, while his tail thumped into my leg. But it wasn't my normal leg. This one was covered with fur and filled with lean muscle. I'd done it! This was getting easier and faster.

I closed my eyes to do one more thing, and just like that, I felt the weight of body armor envelop me. I was just as protected as Faellin now.

I sniffed the air around me, trying to get past the car smells to find Darby's and Pru's scent. Of course, it was Darby's perfume that registered first in my nose. Giving a short 'yap' to get Faellin's attention, I led the way across the parking garage. There was an elevator at the opposite wall.

My nose pressed the elevator button and it opened straight away. The scent of Darby's perfume was stronger here, and I could even pick up a trace of Pru's as well. The elevator panel showed that there were three stories in the building. I hit the button, taking us to the top. No insight there, just hoping for luck to be on our side.

When the door opened, I saw a long hallway with tiled floors and white walls, broken intermittently with doors leading to what I assumed to be offices. Before I could decide whether to go left or right, Faellin took that choice out of my hands. He darted to the right and bounded down the hall. I could smell the scent from my friends grow stronger as we moved.

"Hey! Who let these dogs in here?"

At the shout behind us, Faellin turned. In a flash he was on top of the guy, tearing at his arm that held a gun. At the guy's shrieks of pain, a door opened and two workers dressed in suits rushed to his aid. One tried to grab Faellin to haul him off but Faellin spun and bit his wrist, drawing blood. Seeing the second guy reach into his jacket and pull out a gun, I raced over and tackled him to the ground. A coppery taste filled my mouth when my jaws clamped down on his shoulder.

BANG!

I was thrown against the wall from the gunfire. Despite my body armor, that hurt like hell! My wind was knocked out, but I tried to scrabble back to my feet. Looking up, I stared into the barrel of a gun, held by another man. We froze in place, staring at one another.

"I've got one! Sean! Get the other!"

Time slowed, and I heard the click as the guy prepared to shoot me right in the face. My life passed before me in an instant. But instead of feeling terror at the prospect of dying, it was regret that filled me. What had I ever accomplished in my twenty one years? My parents and friends would miss me, but that was about it. With all the power that was in me as a Celestial, I never got the chance to make a real difference in the world.

Instead of shooting me, the guy holding the gun was thrown sideways, smashing into the tiled wall. He collapsed onto the ground. From behind where he had stood was another man, enormously tall and good looking. He peered at me with eyes that were the color of the sea.

"Lady Bernadette?" he asked. "Or do you be Faellin?"

I shrugged myself up to my feet, taking in every aspect of my rescuer. He was wearing a jumpsuit the color of the ocean. On his chest was a series of wavy lines. This was one of Manaan's soldiers! And he wasn't alone. Another one with ebony skin and equally daunting held the two other goons at bay while Faellin rose to sniff my face.

Hoping that Manaan's guys were talented in catching thoughts, I shouted in my mind. *Two women are being held behind one of these doors. Open all the doors!*

The first guy, the blonde dreamy looking one, nodded.

He raced down the hallway opening every door he came to. A screeching blare of a siren cut through the air before armed guards rounded a corner, bearing down on us with machine guns ready.

Instead of seeking cover, Manaan's guys and Faellin charged at them, all three howling a battle cry. The guards froze, staring at the trio. I was about to join them when I heard Pru's voice.

"Get your hands off me! I'm not going—"

When a loud smack ended her cry, I sprinted to the room where she was. Pru slumped in a chair while some guy was busy unlocking the binding that held Darby. I recognized that broad back and the blond hair. Carl!

I was hardly aware of the vibration and stretching in my body as I morphed back into my human self, my body armor clattering to the floor. I was going to lay a hurting on Carl and when I did; I wanted him to know who had done it. With a snap of my fingers, a stun gun appeared in my palm.

OK, maybe it was wimpy holding a taser instead of an assault rifle or something—especially after I had just been shot myself—but I didn't want to kill anyone if I could avoid it. Don't get me wrong, I was absolutely furious, but I wasn't going to start shooting people if I could help it.

"When you're through untying my friends, you can take their place in the chair, Carl." I smiled when he jumped back and faced me. The look in his eyes seeing me with a stun gun pointed at him was priceless.

But it didn't last long. He held his hands up. "I was trying to help them escape, Bernadette. This isn't right to hold them prisoner. I mean, we're supposed to be the good guys, right? I couldn't go along with this—"

"Save it for someone who might believe you 'cause I don't. On second thought, you're going to be my shield when my friends and I walk out of here. Now finish untying my friends."

"Bernadette! We thought they'd killed you!" Darby leaned to the side, staring at me with tears in her eyes. "You came back to save us!"

But her words fell on deaf ears. I was listening to the grunts and thuds coming from the hall outside. No gunfire or snarls from Faellin. Still watching Carl, I stepped back and peeked down the hall where the platoon of guards had appeared. They were all out cold on the floor while Manaan's guys and Faellin stood over them.

I don't know how they did it but I had new respect for Manaan and his guys, not to mention my dog. Carl straightened and then Darby and Pru pushed by him, coming to my side.

"Faellin!" Pru cried out when she saw the wolfhound.

Darby gawked and then turned to me. "Are they... you know... like you?"

"A little bit." My attention remained on Carl. "Come on! Move it before I change my mind and use this taser on you instead."

Carl's hands rose above his shoulders and he stepped by me, going out into the hallway. "They'll never let you leave, Bernadette. I don't know—

"Put a sock in it, Carl! I'm not interested in anything you've got to say." When Manaan's guys joined us, I projected a command into their heads. *'Get my friends out of this building! I'll go another way with Faellin and try to distract anyone else that's here. This guy's my shield.'*

Pressing the gun into Carl's back, "Move. We're going in the elevator to the parking garage. You're going to drive us out of here." I held onto Faellin's collar with my other hand as we walked quickly down the hall. Behind me, Darby and Pru called out to me before Manaan's guys herded them into the stairwell.

When we were in the elevator, I breathed a sigh of relief, even if it was short lived. There was still the chance that when the door slid open, there would be a troupe of agents waiting there for us. I signaled for Carl to step closer to the door. If there were agents waiting, Carl would be the first to take any fire.

It was tempting to hit the emergency stop button and then transition Faellin and me right out of the building, to get far away from this mess. But I needed to make sure that Manaan's guys and my friends made it out safely.

Carl turned slightly, "There's another entrance to the underground garage. I'd suggest we take it. It'll still be guarded, but there won't be as many. The main focus is gonna be on this elevator." I could see the route in his mind. And considering how terrified Carl was, I was inclined to believe him. When the door opened, Carl called over his shoulder, "Follow me!" before racing out and down the hallway.

Faellin growled, but I urged him forward. "I don't like this either, but it's what we're going to do." We followed Carl, rounding a corner where an exit sign showed at the end of a long hallway.

Carl threw the door open and headed out with Faellin and me on his heels. He called over his shoulder. "The only hope is getting to the trees. They would never let me drive you out of here. This is likely where your friends are going to be, if those guys they're with have any sense."

When we raced down the first set of steps, Carl held his hand out stopping us before we rounded the platform to take the last stairwell. Faellin picked up on the danger as well, bounding from my side and down the stairs.

"No! Faellin!"

Below us, a woman screamed before a burst of gunfire. My heart leapt into my throat! No! I hurried past Carl flew down the set of steps. Faellin's snarls mixed with a man's yelps of pain. I could hardly believe it, seeing Faellin tearing at the guy's leg while a uniformed woman in full riot gear cowered in the corner. The gun she had been using lay at my feet. Somehow Faellin had surprised both of them and now had them disabled, screaming for him to get off.

"Faellin! Come!" I yanked at his collar and then let out a blast of the taser at both of the agents. "Get the door, Carl!" I kicked the spare gun away so that he couldn't grab it on his way by.

But Carl was more interested in getting away from me than scheming some kind of attack. He raced out the door leaving Faellin and me to fend for ourselves. When I poked my head out to check for more guards, I saw Manaan's guys and my friends at the edge of the trees bordering the building. Carl took off, running towards one of the heavy earth-moving machines. But if there were agents stationed nearby, there was no sign of them.

Holding Faellin close, I sprinted across the scrubby landscape, zigzagging in case some sniper had a lock on me. It was only about a hundred feet from the trees. Manaan's guys and Darby yelled to us, urging us to hurry! No urging needed, believe me.

A staccato of machine gun fire, lifted turf next to my feet! Faellin yelped. A quick glance showed a bullet mark on his body armor, but that was all.

"Bernadette!"

My mouth fell open at the sound of my sister Flidais's voice! She stepped out from behind a tree, her hands in flame. Like a baseball pitcher, she leaned back and let loose a volley of fireballs at the machine gunner tucked into the side of the building.

I had only a taser, but my big sis used real firepower. The side of the building and the squad of agents burst into flames. Their screams of pain and surprise barely registered as I ran towards the woods.

Searing pain blasted through my back! It was like a freight train had hit me. I was lifted off my feet, and slammed onto the ground. I rolled onto my back, gasping for breath. I looked down at my chest. Blood was pumping out. I didn't feel any pain, more surprise as I put my hand over the...*hole in me!*

Oh god. I was shot!

Faellin let out a loud bark and then I felt hands tugging at me. My entire field of vision darkened, only that bleeding hole in my chest was visible. Flidais's screams were like they were coming from far away. With every beat of my heart, my life force spilled in a wet pool around me. I was cold... so very cold. I coughed, trying to suck air back into my lungs, but it felt like an elephant was on my chest.

As I lay there, I pictured my parents. And Flidais. She had always wanted to meet my father.

Where was Lugh? I would never see him again.

My last breath gurgled with blood. It tasted horrible.

And everything went black.

Twenty

Flidais

By the stars and moon, I prayed we weren't too late! The forest thinned and I could see a field where Bernadette and the great wolfhound ran.

Half of that fortress was in flames from my fireballs, and Bernadette ran towards us.

"Bernadette!" I called out to her again and saw her look over at me. A staccato of sharp bangs filled the air and Bernadette jerked up into the air. I froze, watching her thud onto the hard ground. Nooooo! These barbarians had hurt my sister! The wolfhound never left her side, tugging at her arm while I raced over to help.

"Gangway!" Lugh's shout beside me caused the earth to shake! He pushed by me and threw himself to the ground beside her.

Before I could get within three feet of her, Angus clapped my shoulder, letting out a war cry. "Death to these barbarians! Come on!"

I felt a whoosh of air beside my face and heard a thud when a projectile ripped through the turf behind me. From the other side of the building, six assailants pointed wicked metal weapons at us. These were the ones who had captured and hurt my sister!

Rage.

A rage I had never felt before swept through me. I felt my scalp tingle with white-hot, hatred.

I've been angry before. I have brought the wrath of a furious Celestial upon those who had tried to invade my forest home. The demi-god Harkness, and his army of almost a thousand soldiers, learned the hard way that angering a Celestial is a fatal mistake. They had rolled into my forest, setting it afire in a crazed attempt to cast me out. Watching trees I had planted with my own hands years and years earlier go up in flames brought out a hatred in me I had never experienced before.

Within minutes, Harkness and all his company were bloated corpses.

That had happened well over a hundred years ago, and since then, the memory of my anger would bring a taste to my mouth.

That fury was a love song compared to the galactic wrath I was to deliver to those who hurt my beloved sister.

Yes, beloved.

There is something special about my Bernadette. I cannot explain what it is—I'm not very well learned. But when she left Otherworld to return to her home, a void in my heart was rent open. I spoke of it to Devi, my mentor from my first days.

She said that hollow thing in my heart was missing a loved one.

And now… her broken and bloody body lay on a battlefield.

I am new to this thing called 'love'. I know not its ways.

MORTAL ENEMIES (Celtic Knot #3)

It is a mystery to me. But I know that the sight of my Bernadette running towards me filled me with such joy.

And when she fell...

I'm not experienced in love.

But I know... oh stars and moons, I know...

How to *hate*.

Ahead of me, Angus fell upon them, but there were many. Too many for his singing blade. He cleaved their armor like a knife through paper, sending bloody limbs flying through the air.

These warriors knew no fear. They rushed at him from all sides in their own mindless blood lust, only to learn of the power of a Fae prince.

Which was nothing to the rage of a Celestial.

I rose into the air above them all, looking down at them. There must have been a company of almost a hundred of these fiends. Angus had thinned their numbers, but I would end it all.

My mind grazed over theirs as they watched me from below. What a disgusting mixture of ignorance, power, lust and joy in battle welled up at me.

Several of them saw me and pointed their weapons at me. Silly children with small toys. They shot my sister in the back; now let them face me.

Staccato flashes from their weapons sent dozens of metal bits at me, faster than an attacking eagle. No matter. I have soared with comets in the night sky, danced with falling stars...

"Boil." I said, waving my hand at the group of enemies.

With a cold, freezing pleasure I watched as the entire company, as one, shrieked in agony. Their single cry of fear and pain matched the agony in my heart over Bernadette. I had made the very blood in their bodies boil in an instant. They all turned scarlet as their bodies melted from the inside.

And fell over dead.

"'Tis done." I said and alighted back to the ground beside Angus.

"I would have beaten them, Lady Flidais," he said.

"You're welcome, Angus," I replied with a scowl.

Turning, I saw Lugh waving his powerful staff over Bernadette's chest. Oh no! She wasn't just injured she was...

I ran towards them, sinking down on Bernadette's other side. I cupped her cheeks in my hands, gazing down into her lifeless eyes.

"Bernadette! Come back to us!" When there was no response, I looked over at Lugh. "Why isn't your magic working? She should breathe by now!"

He shook his head, but the look in his eyes showed pure anguish. "I don't know! I'm trying! Please, I command all the power of the earth, the air and water, flow into her! Wake, sweet Bernadette!" He rocked back and forth, chanting while continuing to wave his staff over her body.

"Lugh! Let me close her wounds." Angus settled in next to Lugh and his hands slid under her body.

She had lost so much blood! The ground was saturated with it! When Angus pulled his hands back, they were coated. Tears flowed down my cheeks as I peered at Bernadette. There was absolutely no sign of life, not even a twitch. We were too late. I had failed my poor little sister.

Angus's voice was sharp when he nudged me. "Do not give up hope, Flidais! Hope is our most powerful ally."

Faellin stood straddling Bernadette's legs, prodding her thigh with his nose and whining.

I swallowed hard and whispered, "Hope and *love*, Angus. It has to work!" The words which Lugh chanted were ancient but familiar to me. They echoed in my head, becoming a prayerful mantra. My poor little sister. She should have stayed in Otherworld with me. Why had I treated her so badly that she'd left? If I could change that, I would in a heartbeat.

"Sing, Flidais. There is power in the song of a Celestial.

Please."

My eyes met Lugh's, and I began the song which Bernadette had sang to rouse him from an ancient spell. The air around us swirled with ribbons of light the more I sang. It became tangible, infusing each of us until we practically glowed. It also filtered into Bernadette.

The trees shake, their leaves
fall like tears
Moonbeams fade, stars shatter
in space
I remember your smile, your
strength and your fear
Days in the sun when we
danced and we sang
And fell together in a meadow
of flowers
You lay with me then, your
touch sweet as rain
Sweet as rain, sweet as rain,
gentle rain
Memories of you enlighten my
heart
Still I long for the day when we
will meet again
Time is the veil that keeps us
apart.

It seemed to go on forever until Bernadette's eyes fluttered. I heard the sharp intake of air and her eyes opened.

Oh my stars.

I sat back on my haunches, my hand covering my mouth in wonder.

And burst into a wailing keen of tears. Like a Banshee, I rocked back and forth, reaching out with one hand, to trace the side of my beloved sister's face.

Oh my stars…

Lugh let out a bellow of joy that shook the earth. "Bernadette! Gods and stars, you're alive!" He gathered her into his arms, cradling her like a newborn. She was so slight beside his fearsome brawn, and yet, they looked a perfect match. He clasped her saying over and over, "Bernadette! Sweet Bernadette. What would I have done if I lost you?"

The women who I'd seen when we first arrived, along with two demi-gods, stood over us. The tall one with the chocolate complexion spoke first. "Is she…" Her eyes went wide, and she grasped the shorter one. "She's alive, Darby!"

I looked at them and held my tongue. She had died, but I wasn't going to get into that, not with humans. They would have no idea what I was talking about. Turning to Manaan's soldiers, I gave them an order. "We must get my sister to safety so she can recover fully."

At Bernadette's touch on my arm, I stared at her. Her lips moved, but it took a few tries before words came out. "No. Everyone, please. You must act as if I am dead. Carry me to the forest and then we can transition out of this place. They must think I'm dead. It's the only way I know that will keep my family safe."

After all my poor sister had gone through, I could care less about these humans. All of them deserved to die.

The tall dark girl spoke again. "She's right. They're watching and they will never stop. They've used us and her family as weapons against her. This is the only way."

My jaw clenched tight, and I stood up. "I'll make them pay. This will end right now. No more threats and hurting my sister!"

Angus reached for my arm before I could set off to kill everyone who could harm Bernadette. "No Flidais. I know how you feel. I'd love to pulverize the lot of them, but Bernadette's friends have been through this with her. They know, and so does Bernadette. Control yourself for

Bernadette's sake, if for nothing else."

I looked over at Lugh. He nodded and stood, still holding Bernadette up in his arms. "It will be clearer later, Flidais. If it comes to destroying these thugs, you'll take a place behind me. For now, we honor Bernadette's wishes."

I stood silently for a moment, gazing back at that building where she'd been held. With just a thought, I could make that place an inferno and it would give me pleasure to do just that. But for now, I'd bide my time. When I turned I saw that the shorter girl, the fair skinned one with the black hair had looped her arm through Angus's walking towards the forest.

What the blazes? She acted like she *knew* him. Who was this woman? I probed her mind.

Oh my stars... She had lain with him? With Angus?

MY ANGUS?

A new rage filled me. This was not familiar to me. I was furious because Angus found this human attractive? But I had cast him away, I had no business with being jealous!

And to be jealous for the affections of a Fae? What was the matter with me!

A fresh wave of anger rolled over my heart. He prefers the charms of a *human*?

Oh, my stars.

Before I lost control, I turned back to the building where they had fled from. I held my hands out before me.

"Fall!" I snarled.

The fortress shuddered, and like a house of cards, fell onto itself in a cloud of dust.

I took a deep breath. At least I got some of it out of my system, no? I nodded sharply at my handiwork of destruction and death and turned back to follow the rest to the woodland.

There was another friend of Bernadette's—Prudence, I believe is her name; ebony skinned and lithe. She walked slowly on her own, head down as if the weight of the world were on her shoulders. Manaan's men stood at the edge of the trees, waiting. I sighed and took off after them. My bowed head conveyed sorrow even though inside I was a cauldron of rage. Someone would pay for what they'd done to my sister.

How dare they do this! The more I thought about how close I'd come to losing her, the angrier I got. I looked over at the gigantic metal machines that looked like enormous insects. My hands whipped up, throwing thunderbolts of lightning at each and every one of them. It was mildly satisfying to see them hurtle through the air and then explode into pieces. Dust and dirt clouded the air, and I rubbed my hands together, shedding myself of this place.

When I got to the forest, the short girl, Darby, peered at me. "What'd you do that for? It wasn't bad enough that the place will be crawling with police and people from the gunfire, but you had to add explosions? I guess subtlety isn't your strong suit. I just want to get out of here in one piece before the whole world descends on us."

I leaned in closer, practically nose to nose with her when I barked. "Let them! Bring it on, I say! I'd love to destroy this whole blasted race of humans for what they did to Bernadette."

At the sound of Bernadette's voice, I rushed to where she lay in Lugh's arms. She grabbed my shoulder, pulling herself near to my ear. "We have to get out of here. Darby's right, but so were you. Good call destroying that building."

Never mess with a Celestial or her sister.

When I returned to my sister's side, I took the hand that Angus extended. It was time to leave this devastation. I heard Bernadette's hoarse whisper asking Lugh to take us to Manaan's ship.

Angus's hand grasped mine tightly while everyone else, along with Faellin grouped together. The air began to swirl and grow lighter as Lugh chanted. It didn't take long before we were inside Manaan's vessel.

132

MORTAL ENEMIES (Celtic Knot #3)

Thank the stars and moons that Angus, Lugh and I had decided to transition together when we heard about Bernadette. If we'd gone in Manaan's ship we may have been too late.

But we wouldn't be in the ship long if I had my way. The only place safe for Bernadette was in Otherworld.

Twenty One

Bernadette

Every move I made caused a shooting pain in my back. Even though I knew it was mostly mended, thanks to Angus's healing touch, that bullet wound still caused severe pain. I took a seat at the table Manaan had set up in his ship. Lugh sat next to me, while Flidais stood in the corner with her arms crossed over her chest.

I had to suppress a smile, watching Prudence and Darby openly gape at the walls and floor of the ship. I remembered my first time on Manaan's magical ship. Looking at the both of them, I spoke, "I was floored the first time I entered Manaan's ship. I know how you're feeling being here."

Darby took a break from openly gawking at her feet sinking deeper into the floor of the ship and glanced over at me. "I feel like I'm walking on a jumping castle at a carnival!"

Prudence reached out, and her fingertips glided gently over the wall beside her. "It's rippling. It's like this thing is alive, like it's breathing or something. And yet, it's completely invisible from the outside."

Manaan, standing at the other end of the table, rapped his knuckle on its surface, interrupting my friends. "Bernadette, let me start by telling you how happy we all are that you survived. I know you risked your life to save your family and friends."

Prudence blurted, "We were so worried, Bern! We thought we'd lost you for sure."

I smiled at her and then turned my attention to Manaan. "How about my parents? Your men are still guarding them?" The government agents had said that they had my parents, but hopefully they'd been lying. Everything from now on depended on my parents being okay.

Manaan nodded. "They are in a small lodging in the mountains. There was a skirmish when a handful of thugs tried to run their vehicle off the road, but my people got them to safety. They're safe now."

"Good. But my parents can't know that I'm alive, not for a while. When the police see the damage from the explosion, it will look like I didn't survive. It's the only way that my family will be safe, if I'm out of the picture." I looked over at Flidais. "Your temper may have helped explain my disappearance."

Darby interrupted, "But what about Pru and me? Do we have to be included in the casualty count? I'm too young to die, Bern."

Prudence shook her head. "But *Bernadette's* isn't too young? No Darby. We escaped. There needs to be someone left to tell what happened. We were there and survived. I'm not sure that they'll believe us but—"

"Please don't mention anything about my powers or that

I'm a Celestial. Give them a short version of the truth. We were abducted, and we had no idea who took us or why. Let the police try to figure it out." I smirked. "Good luck with that."

Flidais walked over and took a seat next to Pru. "Bernadette, if your parents are safe, why not leave here? We could be back in Otherworld in an instant, away from all this treachery."

"Maybe because of *us*?" Darby scowled at Flidais. "If Bloomstein or those Feds aren't convinced that Bernadette is dead, then they're going to come after us and her parents, looking for her. I thought we explained that to you. Why don't you just be quiet and listen to the rest of Bernadette's plan?"

I tried not to gasp hearing the scorn being directed at Flidais, by a *mortal* no less. And the look on my sister's face would be funny if it wasn't so scary.

Flidais snapped back at Darby. "Who are you to tell me what to do? You're less than a gnat I'd squash if you weren't a friend of Bernadette's."

"Not just Bernadette's, but Angus's friend as well for your information!" Darby's shoulders wiggled a bit, looking down her nose at my sister. She smiled and gazed at Angus.

For his part, Angus's lips twitched watching the two females spar. At a nudge from Lugh, he cleared his throat and his voice was serious when he spoke. "Flidais, I know you mean well. We are all concerned about Bernadette and her loved ones here. But this is a totally different culture than what we know. We must bow to Bernadette and her friends' knowledge, to keep them safe."

Whew! A major catastrophe between my sister and Darby averted. "Exactly, Angus. One problem which might work out for us is the secrecy of these organizations who tried to get me to work with them. They're not likely to want any attention from the police." Looking over at Pru and Darby, I continued.

"You need to break it to my parents you saw me shot down before everything exploded. You fled for your lives, barely escaping, so you have no idea what happened after that, except that you knew I was dead."

"That's going to be difficult, Bern. How are—"

"We *have* to, Darby! You said it yourself. If they think she's alive, then they'll come for us too. It's not going to be easy, seeing your mom and dad when we tell them this, Bernadette." Prudence looked down at the table before wiping a tear away.

Manaan spoke next. "Darby and Prudence, you will be escorted and protected by my guards when you go to Bernadette's parents. You won't be captured and tortured for information, not on my watch. I haven't survived for more than a millennium for being too nice, not when it matters."

"Thank you, Manaan. I knew I could count on you. I will visit my parents in time and they will know the truth. I may have to set them up in a new country with new identities, along with my brother of course." Seeing the look on Darby's face, I added. "That goes for you and Pru as well. You name the spot and I'll make it happen. It's the least I can do."

"I can't go with you? I'd like to see this Otherworld. Maybe I'll like it." Darby sniffed and then her gaze rested on Angus again.

Lugh took a deep breath. "You are all invited to my kingdom to visit or live there if you'd like. That goes for your family as well, Bernadette. It may be the simplest solution to all of this."

I looked over at him, wondering how that would work. It had been hard putting up with his chauvinism when I was there. How would my parents and friends—all of whom were mortal — manage living with gods and demi-gods? "We'll see about that later. Lugh. Thanks for your offer."

Prudence looked over at me. "When do we tell your

parents? Where are you going to be?"

Practical and smart as usual, Prudence cut to the chase. I sighed and my heart ached telling her this, "As soon as you've got something to eat and a moment to catch your breath, you should go. This has to happen quickly, Prudence. We're counting on you. But we won't be far away."

I closed my eyes for a moment and when I opened them, there were three cell phones in my palm. "Take these and call me. I doubt very much if any calls from these can be traced by those agents or Bloomstein." When I created them, I made them so they could only call the other phone. Sorry, Verizon!

Angus cleared his throat. "Bernadette, I will go with Darby and Pru. If I transition with them, it would be faster and safer." He looked at Manaan, "No offense Manaan, but my powers are greater than your men's."

"What?" Flidais eyes practically bulged, glaring at Angus. "Why would you suggest going with them?" Her eyes became flinty when she added. "If a greater being is needed to aid these women, then it will be me."

Lugh's eyes met mine before he spoke. Yes, he had picked up on Flidais's jealousy as well. "Why don't *both* of you go? Bernadette will be fine with me. We will join you in a day or two."

My smile was grim when I looked at Angus and Flidais. "Yes, both of you safeguard my friends. And as Lugh said, it won't be long before we join you. I wouldn't want to miss my *funeral*. There'd better be lots of flowers and mourners." And my parents and Seth, heartbroken. Even though picturing that was an arrow in my chest, I couldn't see any other way of protecting them than to pretend that I had died.

Manaan clapped his hands and my eyes widened seeing the table set with fruit, meat dishes, vegetables and jugs of beverages. It looked wonderful and smelled even better. But my appetite was the last thing on my mind.

"Eat! Help yourself." Manaan gave my shoulder a squeeze before he filled goblets with the juice he'd conjured. "I know you normally don't eat, Angus and Flidais, but I would suggest you partake. You will need every ounce of your strength and power." He looked at me from under his bushy white eyebrows. "That goes for you too, Bernadette."

A quick glance at Pru and Darby showed their shock at seeing all the food magically appear. My poor friends. Since I'd returned home, they'd not only had their lives upended and threatened, but their sense of reality had taken a hit as well. I put my hand over Pru's, "I'm really sorry for all the crap I've brought into your lives."

It was Darby who answered, helping herself to a leg of chicken. "It hasn't been dull, that's for sure. I won't miss getting kidnapped, although I hate that you won't be around. I wonder if Nosy Natalie rented our apartment?"

I shook my head. "Whatever happens, you'll never have to live there, Darby. I will leave you well provided for." I couldn't imagine how awful Natalie would make their lives if they had to come crawling back for a place to live.

She smirked at me. "I'm thinking New Zealand might be a sweet place to hang out for a while. If you set me up there, I'll consider the score even." Flashing Angus a warm smile, she added. "Once I'm settled maybe, I'll have a party and you can visit me."

Lugh spoke before Flidais could comment. "That sounds good. I'm sure all of us would enjoy that. Imagine, no battles or running from scoundrels who are trying to use you for their own end. Bernadette and I will be sure to visit. It sounds like someplace you'd enjoy, Flidais."

Pru pulled out her phone after she'd eaten half her plate of food. "It's almost nine o'clock. We should get going soon, much as I hate what we're going to have to do."

Manaan leaned into Angus, "I'll give you the exact coordinates of the place where Bernadette's parents are. It's called Mountain View Resort, room 14."

"Thank you for your kindness, Manaan" Flidais stood up. "With luck, we will be back in a few days." Looking over at me, she smiled. "Stay out of trouble, little sister."

Pru rushed over and hugged me. "I second that, Bern. I'll call you to let you know how things are going. When will I see you again?"

I pulled back and gazed into her eyes. "After my funeral. We have to wait to make sure you aren't being watched, but it will be as soon as I can do it."

Darby had risen, waiting to also give me a parting hug. "We'll get a nice place on the beach down under and this will be a horrible memory. Thinking of that is how I'm getting through this."

I gave her a hug and whispered in her ear. "Ease up on flirting with Angus. Flidais and he had a fight, but I know there are still feelings between those two. You don't want to mess with her, Darby."

She pulled back and winked. "We'll see about that." Turning to Angus, she continued. "Anytime you're ready, Fae Prince."

Uh oh. But Flidais didn't rise to the bait, taking Pru's hand and then reaching for Angus's. "I'm anxious to see your earth family, Bernadette, although it will be from a distance."

I watched the four of them stand close together and then disappear in the blink of an eye.

That was that. My poor parents and Seth. It broke my heart knowing how this would hurt them.

Twenty Two

T he next day, I paced the small confines of the ship with the cell phone in my hand. Neither Pru nor Darby had called, and considering they'd left shortly after they ate the night before, they would have been in touch with my parents by this time. I tried calling them more than a few times, but there hadn't been any answer, which added to my worry.

Lugh looked up from where he sat on the floor, rubbing Faellin's chest. "It does no good to wear your feet off worrying like this, Bernadette. If there were trouble, I'm sure we would have heard by now. Come sit with me."

As tempting as the offer was, I knew I couldn't sit idly by. "Why don't we go there, Lugh? I can disguise myself. We'll leave Faellin here with Manaan. I just need to see that they're all right. Plus, Flidais is no fan of Darby's. Who knows what she'll do if Darby keeps flirting with Angus?"

He sighed and then rose to his feet. Pulling me into his arms, he murmured. "I hate this waiting as much as you, Bernadette. If it were up to me we'd all be in Otherworld right now. There might be a lot of war and battles in my homeland, but at least there aren't greedy bastards threatening women. And for what? To acquire powers that they have no understanding of?"

I looked up at him. "I know. But I have to see that things are going as planned. What's going on there?"

Manaan looked over from where he sat at the table. "I don't think you have a choice here, son. Go with her, but both of you should be careful. Just check things out and return at once. Either that or allow my men to go to check on them."

I shook my head. "No. It has to be me. I *know* what *should* be happening at this point. No one else can understand that. But what I can't explain is why Darby or Pru haven't called."

"Does that thing even work inside this craft? Maybe they *have* tried to contact you, but it didn't come through." Lugh took the phone from my hand and scowled at it. "I'd trust a raven more than this gadget."

"You might be right about the phone. This is a magical vessel, after all." I started off towards the bathroom. "I'm going to change my hair color and style. And try some new clothes. Give me five and I'll be right back. Then we're going to see how things are with my parents."

I went into the bathroom and ran my fingers through my hair, gazing into the mirror. Blonde or brunette? What the hell? I'd go with a blonde pixie style. I closed my eyes for a few moments and when I opened them, I hardly recognized the stranger gazing back at me. Gone were my long locks of fiery red hair, replaced with a spiky blond cut. It was actually cute, if I did say so myself.

Next, my clothes. I conjured up a blue maid's uniform. It

was sad to say, but being a service worker in drab working clothes would me a cloak of invisibility. I wasn't sure how Lugh would feel about dressing as a gardener or garbage man, but he'd just have to suck it up. The finishing touches were sets of eyeglasses.

When I emerged from the bathroom, Lugh's eyes widened before he burst out laughing. "You look like one of those workers in that hotel we stayed in." Seeing my mouth clamp shut, he added, "Still gorgeous though. No matter what you wear or do to your hair, you're still beautiful."

"I see your survival skills are as good as ever, Lugh." I closed my eyes and then handed him a set of coveralls. "These are for you. And the eyeglasses too. Put them on."

Of course, Lugh being Lugh, didn't bother to change in the bathroom but stripped down right there in front of Manaan and me. Hell, it reminded me of the first time I'd set eyes on him, prancing around in his birthday suit. Not that I minded. Oh...Not. At. All. Be still my heart.

When he was dressed, I took his hand. Turning to Manaan, I smiled, "We'll return in a few hours. If we aren't back by then, please send help. It's not Paul's uncle or the psycho billionaire I'm worried about, it's those government clowns."

"Tell me how magnificent I look." Lugh stood tall in all his six foot six glory, preening in the drab green coveralls, wearing dark-rimmed eyeglasses and a baseball cap.

I took his hands in mine and went up on tippy toes to give him a quick kiss. "Perfect. But you'll have to dial the arrogance down, Lugh. Play this very low key."

He bowed his head. "It is difficult to hide my magnificence but I will follow your lead, Bernadette. Now, let us go."

I had a general idea of where my parents were but tried to focus in on the exact directions which Manaan had supplied. We held hands, and I pictured them in the motel room. After a few minutes, the familiar swirling of lights and the nausea started rumbling in my gut. The vibrations began in my fingers and extended all the way to the top of my head before my feet bumped into something hard.

Opening my eyes, I saw that we had landed next to a dumpster. On one side of it a long narrow building extended with two stories with small balconies at each of the units. It was a motel, but was it the one where my parents were? I'm still new at this mode of transportation—I remember feeling overwhelmed the first time I got behind the wheel of a car; that's *nothing* compared to teleporting.

"Bernadette!"

I froze for a moment before I recognized my sister's voice. She and Angus stood just beyond us at the edge of a line of trees and shrubs. She was still wearing the clothes which she normally wore at home in the forest, a tunic and sandals with laces that criss-crossed her calves. I'd have to suggest something else for her. And Angus too, in his rough hewn kilt and shirt. In all the commotion yesterday, I'd never given it a thought.

Lugh grabbed my hand, and we made a beeline for the tall shrubs. "What happened? Where are Prudence and Darby?"

Angus glanced at Flidais before he answered. "They're all still inside. Your friends stayed the night. We've been keeping watch on the building. There haven't been any suspicious people hanging around."

I thought for a few moments and then I spoke. "I'm going to try calling them again. I have to find out how my parents are doing." I pulled the phone out of my pocket and hit the number for Pru. It rang for a few times before she answered.

"Bernadette! I've tried to call you about twenty times!" she hissed in a whisper.

I looked over at Lugh; he'd been right about the ship interfering with the phone. "How are they, Pru? Are they returning home today?"

"They were heartbroken. That was the worst thing I've *ever* had to do. Your mother practically fainted when I told them about you."

I felt my gut drop even lower than it had been picturing my mom's face. And Dad's. "Have you spoken to them today?"

"Darby went to grab coffee to take it to them." There was a pause and a thud in the phone before she added. "Hang on. She's back."

The next voice I heard was Darby's. "They're leaving to meet your brother at their house. We haven't seen your sister or Angus since we arrived."

"They're here. Lugh and I decided to come and see for ourselves when we didn't hear from you. What did Dad say? He's not going to the police, is he?"

"We tried to convince him not to, but he said he *has* to. There isn't a body and no proof aside from our word that we saw you struck down. There has to be an investigation in order to get a death certificate, which the funeral home needs in order to do the service and—"

"Shit!" Again, I looked at Lugh wondering if perhaps if he was right again. Maybe taking everyone to Otherworld would be the only way to fix this mess. But I knew my parents would hate it, not to say anything of my brother Seth.

There was no other way around it. There were official channels that had to be followed in a death. I was glad that Flidais had demolished the site, but now maybe that idea wasn't the best one in the world.

"Okay." I had to concede. "Thanks for offering to drive my folks home, Darby. Angus and Flidais will be close by in case those government dudes or Bloomstein shows up. Maybe staying with my folks for a bit wouldn't hurt."

"Well, we've got nowhere else to go, do we? Our apartment in the Bronx is gone and Paul's relatives are probably all watching the apartment in Soho." Darby sounded miffed and a little whiny.

"It's just for a few days, Darby! Then you can go to Soho. That apartment is paid for. We need to show all of them that I'm gone... as in dead. We'll get together later and sort out where you'll live, as I said yesterday."

Darby must have handed the phone back to Pru as it was she who spoke next. "Don't worry about us, Bernadette. I'm more sorry for your parents. I think it's a good idea to stay close to them for a few days, to help them through this."

"Thanks, Pru. I'll be in touch later. The phone doesn't work on Manaan's ship. Take care." With that, I hung up. I turned to Angus and Flidais. "You need to stay close. Go to my folks' home and keep watch for any suspicious people hanging round." Before I turned to Lugh, I added. "You two might want to change your clothes first. Try to fit in."

"Are you ready to return to Manaan's ship, Bernadette?" Lugh looked down at me and then took my hand.

"No. Not yet. Let me sneak a peek at my parents. Let's go to the front of the building and watch for them." I signaled for Angus and Flidais to come with us and then started off to round the building.

Lugh was at my side, "So I'll finally get to see your parents. This isn't the way I'd hoped for but…"

I looked up at him. "I know. This just totally sucks. Your first impression of my parents is where they're in mourning for me. How crazy is that?"

He shook his head slowly. "Meeting your family has always been a challenge."

I nodded. "Yeah. But at least it isn't my biological mother who tried to kill you!"

"Life is never dull around you, Bernadette. But I can't imagine life without you either. So I'm trapped, even though I no longer owe you a life debt." He smiled, and I felt my heart melt. He could make my knees weak with just a look.

"Does that mean you're asking me to marry you? You'll have to do better than that, if it is." I smirked, gazing up at him as we rounded the building.

"That depends, Bernadette. Would I get my dog back? I would sweep you off your feet if that was part of the deal." He grinned at me and then pulled me in to plant a kiss on my forehead.

I was about to come back with a smartass remark, but I saw the door to room 14 open and my father stepped out. God. They looked like hell. When had they grown so old? My death had extinguished any spark of life in them. Even my mother's hair was a rat's nest, which was totally out of character.

Lugh leaned down and whispered in my ear as we hunched close to the building. "I wish you'd be honest with them and ask them to come to my world. They don't look well, Bernadette. This is killing them."

For a moment I agreed with him. What was the point of doing all this if it was having such a terrible effect on the people I loved? It was tempting to call out to them and rush over. My heart actually hurt watching them walk over to the car, joining Darby and Pru.

"Hey! Mother of Bernadette! Bernadette's father! Wait!"

My mouth fell open, and I watched with horror as Lugh strode forward. He looked back at me and grabbed my hand, pulling me along after him. "Come on! I can't bear to see your parents like this. I am Lugh, Tuatha de Danaan. I will fix this!"

Oh, my god.

Twenty Three

I watched my mother's eyes change from a narrow look of curiosity at this brute of a man, dressed in workman's clothes approaching her, to becoming wide eyed seeing me beside him. She actually staggered, clutching her chest as she gaped at me.

But then her face lit up and her eyes welled with tears. "Bernadette? It's really you? I can't believe this!" Breaking away from my father, she flew over. She collapsed in my arms, hugging me until I was practically breathless. "Bernadette! Oh my poor, poor girl! I can't believe this! Thank *god*, you're alive!"

"You're welcome!" Lugh murmured.

I tried not to laugh at Lugh's response when I pulled back. Tears flowed down my mother's face as she clutched me once more, like she'd never let go. She was a bleary mess, but totally the woman who loved me. My father joined us, openly sobbing as he hugged me close.

"We thought you were dead, Bernadette! Why did your friends tell us you were? I wanted to die as well!" But when he eased back to look at me his eyes were sad. "Why would you do such a thing to us? Why Bernadette? Your mother and I—"

"I'm sorry, Dad! I was trying to protect you!"

By this time Darby and Pru had wandered over. "Bernadette? What the hell? This makes no sense. You told us to pretend you were dead and then you do this? Why did you—"

"Enough!" Lugh towered over them. "Bernadette is here with her parents and that is all that matters. This nonsense of being captured and chased by these mortals has got to stop! I will not allow this to continue." Lugh pulled himself to his full height, looking down his nose at everyone. He looked every inch the god he truly was.

For once, I was happy that he'd taken this decision out of my hands. Since I'd been home, I'd made a mess of things.

"Who the hell are you?" My father's face was pinched, looking up at Lugh. Even though Dad was tall, he looked small next to Lugh's brawny figure.

"I am Lugh, Tuatha de Danaan, ruler of Otherworld! At last we meet, father of Bernadette." He took my mother's hand and bent lower to kiss it. "Enchanted to meet you, dear mother of Bernadette. You are much more pleasant than her first mother who I encountered. At least you aren't trying to kill me and conquer my kingdom!"

Seeing the confusion in my parents' faces, I inserted myself between Lugh and them. "This is the god I told you about. He came to my rescue when the government jerks took us. They used you and my friends as threats to make me help them. When I tried to escape, they shot me. I actually was dead. Lugh brought me back to life."

"Good lord!" My mother's hand went to her heart again, and she slumped lower. "It was *true* what your friends said? You died?" She turned to my father. "Lanny. I need to sit down. I can't believe all this. Our daughter died and now she's back. I swear this girl will be the death of us both."

I rushed to her side, steadying her. I never saw Angus and Flidais approach until Flidais spoke. "Lugh wasn't the only one who came to help Bernadette. I am Flidais, Bernadette's sister. This is Angus Mac Og, Fae Prince."

When I looked over at them I saw that they had also chosen to wear a maid's uniform and workman's clothes. Even so, they looked regal with their heads held high.

My father's mouth opened and closed a few times before he managed to get any words out. "You... you look just like my Bernadette! You're from that place too? That Otherworld?"

My mother almost leapt from my arm to grasp Flidais and pull her into a hug. "Thank you! Thank you for helping my daughter! How can we ever repay you?"

Flidais grinned, but there were tears in her eyes when she spoke. "You already have, dear lady. My own mother never showed as much affection for me as you just did. I have wanted to meet you since the time Bernadette told me about her Earth family."

My father shook Angus's hand and then turned to Flidais. "*You* are part of our family now. Imagine! Me, a schmuck from Westchester having two goddesses as daughters."

Angus cleared his throat. "This is all very nice, Bernadette, but what about the forces lined up against you? Should we be standing out here? I'm not frightened for my own safety, but what about your parents and friends?"

Flidais swatted him on the chest, her eyes electric. "Let them come! I welcome their attack!"

My forehead knotted watching my sister's outburst. Flidais went into warrior mode with very little provocation since coming to Earth. For someone who liked the peace of the forest, she certainly didn't shy from defending her loved ones.

My father started to say something but then his eyes became wide looking down the street. I turned and saw three black SUV's pull into the parking lot of the motel.

My breath froze in my chest watching them park. They'd found us.

Twenty Four

T hat's them? I will turn them into dust. They will wish they'd never been born!" Flidais had her hand raised high.

Before she could lob off a fireball, I grabbed her. "No. Wait. We can't just vaporize them here in broad daylight." I watched the door open and men in black suits get out. One of them opened the back door of the first vehicle and I openly gaped, seeing Bloomstein emerge.

Even though the men weren't holding guns, I knew they were armed. I'd had some experience being around them. "What do you want? How'd you find me?" I directed my question at Bloomstein, who sauntered casually over to where we stood.

"Is that any way to greet me? Where are your manners, Bernadette? Allow me to introduce myself Mr. and Mrs.

Adelson. I'm Wesley Bloomstein." He looked over at Flidais, Angus and Lugh giving them the once over. It was odd, but he actually looked cheery, with a bounce in his step.

"You won't get me to cooperate with you any longer, Bloomstein. I'm done being your guinea pig or anyone else's. You might as well leave before you get hurt." I could hardly stand the sight of him. And hearing Lugh's angry sigh beside me, I wasn't the only one.

"As I told you many times, I have no wish to hurt you or be hurt. I want you and me to partner, and actually do something to make this world better. That seems like a reasonable thing to do."

"Just say the word, Bernadette and I will destroy him and his minions. They have tried my patience too long, threatening you and your family." Lugh's voice was deadly calm, staring at Bloomstein.

I held my hand against Lugh's chest. "Wait." Peering hard at Bloomstein, I continued. "How did you know where to find me?" If he knew I was here, the government agents might not be far behind.

He sighed, "Have you never heard of microchips? When you were unconscious, we implanted one under your skin. I lost you for a little while, but then you surfaced again. If you hadn't broken out of that facility we were going to remove you from there. The feds are always concerned about weapons and war. My plans for you would actually help people as opposed to kill them."

I got right in his face when I blurted my response. "You kidnap me and my friends, threaten my family and *you're* the good guy in this? Are you nuts? I'm not buying it. You want me to help you prolong your life."

Flidais stepped over and grabbed Bloomstein's lapels with her fists. "You laid hands on my sister? You must die for your treachery."

My heart almost stopped seeing the six henchmen reach

in their jackets and aim hand guns at all of us. "No, Flidais! This is over, Bloomstein. Take your men and leave us alone. But mark my words, if you ever threaten my family again, you're dead meat. I will personally roast you alive."

Flidais shoved Bloomstein back before she removed her fists from his coat. "You're a worm that should be crushed under my foot."

He glared at my sister for a moment before signaling with a hand wave for his men to put their weapons away. Brushing his coat lightly, his voice was casual. "As you wish. But..." He glared at me, "...it had always been my intention to protect your parents and friends. There is so much potential in you Bernadette to change longevity. The possibilities of harnessing your power to ease the climate problems are endless. We would rule the world with that. I regret my actions in being so heavy-handed with you. I can see there is much more to your power than I'd originally thought."

I didn't yet breathe a sigh of relief. This was a wily fox with lots of tricks up his sleeve. "So you want everyone to believe that your intentions are altruistic. Sorry, but I'm not a fool. Even though there are probably lots of other people who would believe you. And you'd stand to profit by that. That's why you want me to work with you."

He smiled. "Some would accuse me of being overly cautious. But it's been my experience that taking that extra step has always paid off. I had hoped we could be partners. No matter. I have your blood samples and DNA. Your blood has given me a new lease on life."

The reason for his smugness became clear. And it wasn't just me who'd picked up on it.

Flidais once more stepped closer to him, threatening him with proximity. "You have fed on my sister's blood. That is sorcery of the worst kind. You must die for that."

Lugh nudged Flidais aside and lifted Bloomstein up, swinging him high into the air. The thugs spread out, firing their guns at Lugh. But none of the bullets reached his body. Angus was a literal whir holding a steel shield between Lugh and Bloomstein's guys. Flidais wasted no time in disarming all of them with a bolt of energy from her fingertips. All their weapons were twisted scrap metal scattered on the ground.

So much for Bloomstein's men; their loyalty only went so far. As one, they scrambled, racing to the vehicles and hightailing it out of there, leaving a dust cloud from the spinning tires. Meanwhile Bloomstein wailed, pleading for mercy as Lugh continued to swing him like a rag doll.

Lugh glanced at me, "Where do you want him to land, Bernadette? That tree over there or on the roof of that building? That should finish this piece of decrepit filth for once and for all."

My father surprised me when he spoke. "Stop! Don't add to this senseless death and violence. Please put him down, Lugh."

Lugh stopped swinging the old man, holding him still while he stared at my father. "I don't know about here, but anyone who drinks blood or eats the flesh of a fellow creature is abhorrent... an abomination."

Prudence stepped from where she had stood next to Darby. "Technically, he didn't drink it. He's using Bernadette's blood to rejuvenate himself. Even so, that can't be allowed to continue."

Bloomstein was practically in tears when he shrieked. "Don't you people understand? She has the power to change life on earth! It's not just the aging process. The potential is limitless! We can harness her power and all of us will profit."

"Put him down, Lugh. We must destroy whatever samples he has taken from me." But even as I said it, I wondered what the government people had done while I slept. Their goal was not to save the world, but to further their power around the globe. The building where they'd taken me might be destroyed, but who knew if they'd safe-guarded blood samples in another location.

Bloomstein landed with a thud, barely keeping his balance when Lugh unceremoniously let him drop. It was mildly satisfying to see him filled with terror and powerless, unlike his usual arrogant self.

His face was the color of a fire engine when he stammered, "Don't do this, Bernadette. Don't you care about what this could mean for your family and future generations? Not to say anything about the wealth it would bring to them?"

"You didn't care about my family when you had me under your thumb. I will not allow you to be some kind of Dr. Frankenstein with my blood. You had no right to do what you did." But it wasn't just the threat of what could happen. I totally didn't like the idea of leaving pieces of myself around to be manipulated... especially by these monsters.

Prudence looked over at me. "What should we do, Bernadette?"

I was silent for a few moments, trying to figure this out. "First thing, you return home with my parents. We continue with pretending I'm dead on the off chance that the government guys haven't also tracked me, like Bloomstein did."

Bloomstein interrupted. "I could help with that. There has to be a police investigation to produce a death certificate. I have important people in my payroll who can see that they don't investigate too thoroughly. Just allow me to continue my work and I promise I won't say anything about you being alive."

Flidais practically spat at him when she hissed. "Quiet! You are in no position to make demands of my sister. I don't know why we don't just finish you right here and now."

Ignoring Flidais, I answered him. "You will help with the

police. In exchange for that we will allow you to live. But your crazy plan is over. We will go with you to your home and ensure that this happens, while my parents continue on with this charade."

My mother came over to me and hugged me, whispering into my ear. "What about your brother? Should we tell him about this, that you're alive?"

I shook my head when I eased back from her. "It is probably best that he doesn't know, for his own safety." I shook my head slowly and with a wan smile, added, "Besides, he would probably have you guys committed if he knew the truth."

Twenty Five

An hour later, Lugh, Angus, Flidais and I arrived with Bloomstein at his estate. It was a gated property in the mountains, probably the Catskills, the upper state area. It was a tight fit in my parents van but it was the only vehicle available, leaving Darby and Pru to call a cab to take my parents back to their place.

I drove down the lengthy drive to the three-story mansion, and glanced over at Lugh. "This is the kind of place that being really rich and powerful buys you in my country."

His smile was grim when he answered. "This world still stinks, Bernadette. The air is filthy, the water and food isn't pure like it is in Otherworld. Why is this man so obsessed with saving himself and it?"

I thought of my parents and friends, even innocent

people who had no responsibility in creating the pollution that threatened our world. "It's worth saving. Although I'm not convinced that Bloomstein is the guy to head up a rescue plan. Guys like him always have a hidden agenda, but with him it's primarily profit and power."

When the car pulled up to the front of the house, Lugh was the first out of it. He flung open Bloomstein's door and yanked him out of the seat by the collar of his suit jacket. Holding him up in the air with one hand, he said, "You are lucky Bernadette is merciful. But don't test my patience anymore than you already have."

Bloomstein let out a squeak and nodded when Lugh lowered him to the ground.

I got out of the vehicle, peering around at the buildings on the estate. I didn't see any other vehicles around, but they could have parked in the enormous garage that sat off to the side of the building. This had been too easy, getting him to agree to destroy the samples. I kept a sharp lookout as I followed Lugh and Bloomstein to the front door.

The old man punched in the security code, and the door swung open. He glanced back at me before entering. "There are only the service staff inside. Although you probably don't believe me."

"You got that right."

Angus stepped by me, "Lugh. I don't like the looks of this. Let me go first." Immediately a steel shield was in his hand as he strode into the house.

But there was nothing. No rain of bullets or people around. Bloomstein was next, followed by Lugh.

Flidais put her hand on my arm, stopping me. "I'm going to shift into a wolf, Bernadette. If this is a trap, and he has more mercenaries waiting to ambush, my senses will pick that up."

I nodded but cautioned her. "He doesn't know that we can shape shift, and it's best to keep it that way. Wait until he is well out of sight before you shift." My gut was tight when I left her on the front step. We could well be stepping into our doom. To make matters worse, Lugh's magical staff was back on Manaan's ship, leaving us exposed if we were attacked and hurt. Or worse yet, killed.

Bloomstein led the way down a long hallway past a set of ornate stairs. I recognized the carpet and the wallpaper from when I'd been brought to have dinner with the old psycho. He hit the button and then his gaze took in the rest of us.

"Where is the other one? Your sister?" For just a moment his guard dropped, and I was able to pick up his thoughts. This *was* a trap and he wanted to ensnare *all* of us.

"She's outside keeping an eye out in case any of your guys show up. You'd better hope for their sake, they don't, or you'll have to hire a whole new gang of them." The elevator opened, and I looked over at Angus. It was clear that he'd picked up on the same thing from Bloomberg.

The sooner we found and destroyed his lab, the better. After that, we'd be out of there. I followed the others into the elevator and silence shrouded us as we descended. Bloomstein's anxious energy practically exuded from his body as we waited. I reached out and hit the emergency stop button.

He jerked back and looked at me. "What are you doing? I thought you wanted to get to the lab."

"She doesn't trust you and neither do we." Lugh towered over the old man, backing him into the corner of the small space. "This is a trap. Do you know what we do to people who try that where I come from?"

Again Lugh lifted Bloomstein with one hand until the old guy's head bumped against the roof of the elevator. "Who else is here? You better tell the truth or your head is going through this contraption."

"I swear it isn't a trap! Put me down and I'll show you!" The old guy looked like he'd have a stroke at any minute. "Please. You must believe me."

Before I could say anything more the elevator jerked and

then continued down. "Lugh! There's got to be someone down there, controlling this thing. Whatever you do, don't let this weasel escape."

The door opened, and my eyes widened. Two guns pointed at me, in the hands of Bloomstein's guards in dark camo clothing. Beside them were another handful of armed mercenaries ready to take us on.

From where his head still pushed against the roof, Bloomstein shouted. "Kill these ruffians, but don't hurt the girl!"

Angus held the metal shield up and rushed out, knocking the two closest thugs off their feet. A spray of bullets banged against the metal before Lugh tossed Bloomstein forward. The old man landed next to the guards, but Lugh was right behind him, charging into the closest guys, banging them into the walls.

When I saw a couple of the others turn to attack Angus, I threw a jolt of electrical current from my fingertips at them. They jerked and then fell to the floor. But Lugh had his hands full as another couple of guys let loose a volley of bullets, even as they edged back, away from him.

"Stars and moons! You dare to assault me!" Lugh kept going, grabbing their guns and tossing them aside like they were toys. He belted the one guy, propelling him about twenty feet down the hall and through a plate-glass window. The other clown scrambled away before Lugh could get him.

A door banged somewhere from where he'd taken off and then a blood-curdling scream followed. There were only a few Bloomstein's guys left standing, but Angus soon changed that.

Bloomstein lay in a fetal position on the floor, covering his head with his bent arms. Lugh stood over him for a moment before plucking him up off the floor. There were holes in Lugh's coveralls and some blood from where he'd taken a couple of hits from the gunfire. Even though he had to be seriously hurt, he kept on, holding Bloomstein up with one hand.

Angus would tend to Lugh's wounds after this was finished. I started forward, "Come on! The lab is just down this hall." I was about to race down there when Flidais rounded the corner.

"So it was a trap. I found four guards at a rear door and then some other enemies racing up the stairs. What do you want to do with the rest of these ruffians?" Flidais looked around at the slumped and unconscious bodies of Bloomstein's guys.

I smiled at her. "Remember that trick Aine did on me with the vines? Try that while we destroy everything that Bloomstein saved in the lab." As I walked by her, I clapped her shoulder. "Don't forget Bloomstein. Make his ropes extra tight."

"With pleasure."

I walked into the lab and saw the test tubes, the machines and paraphernalia that contained my blood. Without another thought, I unleashed a whirlwind of energy that toppled every item, smashing glass and metal into tiny pieces. Just to be on the safe side, I hit it with a wave of heat, as hot as any furnace to destroy and incapacitate everything.

There would be no trace of Bernadette in this lab or anywhere else that could help the geriatric psycho in his schemes.

This was truly over. Let the police investigate all they wanted. They'd never find any of us to prosecute.

Twenty Six

A week later...

Flidais and I sat next to each other on a headstone, watching my funeral. There was no way I could be convinced to stay away, despite Lugh and Angus's protests. When Flidais suggested shifting into house cats, to take the proceedings in from a distance, their argument was over.

She projected a thought over to me. "So that tall, dark-haired male is your brother, Seth? He's cute, even if he is a bit scrawny for my taste."

My tail twitched as I watched the small group gathered. *"Yes. As far as I know he doesn't know the truth, that I'm alive."* He looked pretty shook up, with his arms clasping both my parents close to him, on either side. It was disappointing to see that only about twenty people had shown up for my send-off. But as for secret agents, mafia types or Bloomstein' men, there were none in sight, which was a good thing.

"You don't think you should let your brother know when this ceremony is over? He could go with us to that island your friends chose to live. I'd like to meet him. I would like very much to get to know all of your family."

I looked over at her. She'd never known what it was like to grow up with a mother and father. Aine had never shown the least bit of affection, and not much interest at all in Flidais's life. That is, if you didn't count her plotting and scheming to install Flidais on Lugh's throne.

I sidled closer to her. "You mean you would like to get to know your family, Flidais."

She stiffened beside me, but only for a moment. *"What do you mean?"*

"Mee-owww!" I said aloud in mock frustration. *"Silly kitty! You're my sister, correct?"*

She bobbed her head in agreement.

"And those people are my family. So it stands to reason that they're YOUR family too, doesn't it?"

"I don't think it works like that, Bernadette."

That did it. I batted her with my paw. I hate that phrase! We fell from our perches, mock fighting, rolling over and over on the grass. Finally, I got to my feet, arched my back and hissed at her. *"They're every bit as much YOUR family as they are mine!"*

She put her nose in the air and turned a circle, her tail almost straight up. *"Well... if you insist so strongly, I'll think about it."*

I let out another hiss of frustration and plopped down to continue to watch the service. Poor Seth was completely distraught. *"I think you're right, though, Flidais. I don't think there's much choice about that anymore. Seth has to be told the truth."*

I attempted to chuckle but it came out as a rumbling purr. *"He's pretty uptight even at the best of times but when he finds out I'm a Celestial with crazy-ass powers, it's gonna really short circuit his head. That could be fun, I guess."*

We were silent for a few moments, watching the rabbi leave the head of the grave to say a few words to my parents. Darby and Prudence stood to the side, while my aunts, uncles and cousins bunched close together. It was so strange. I'd wanted to come home so bad when I was in Otherworld and now that I'd returned, I was attending my own funeral. If there had been no place for me in Lugh's world, my experience at home showed that I was even less at home here in New York.

Flidais stretched and then asked, "When you return to Otherworld, will you give it another try with Lugh? You're welcome to live with me if it doesn't work out."

"I don't know how that will play out. At this point, I just want all of this to be over. I'll deal with that later, after my funeral." The truth was that the horror of what we'd all been through was sinking in. Funerals have a way of making things real.

Flidais had read my thoughts. "Think positively, Bernadette. You survived and protected your family and friends. Life is never without challenges. That's what makes things interesting." Her paw came up and she batted my ear, playfully. "But not too many challenges, like the mess that your life here has been."

I bit her foot and made a swipe at her too. This was kind of like the lessons she'd taught me back in her home, the two of us play fighting. *"Speaking of messes, I guess you won't mind when Angus visits Darby. He could help her hang pictures and fix up the home we're going to find for her."*

The next swipe she made at my face hurt. She hadn't pulled her claws in and I took a slash next to my ear. I ignored it and continued baiting her, *"I wonder if he'll take her to Ethereal to see his home."*

She snarled and knocked me off the headstone. We landed in a snarling ball of fur before I leapt to my feet, racing away from her. The scent of lilies and roses filled the crisp air as I ran past the mourners. None of them paid any attention to the two stray cats playing in the graveyard. It had been too long since I'd been able to do this with my sister. It was one of the perks of being Celestials, donning any animal's body to experience life through its eyes.

Finally, we stopped at the edge of the cemetery before the gate which led to the open street. Flidais rolled on her back, rubbing her spine against the hard earth. *"What now, Bernadette? Is this ceremony almost over?"*

"I think so. They'll all go back to my parents' house and continue for the evening. We might as well go back to Manaan's ship. Tomorrow, they'll join us there. I'll call Mom and give her the okay about telling Seth. But I can't promise he'll join them on this get-away to New Zealand."

"I hope he does, but if not, his loss. Let's shift back and then get out of here. I've had enough of your funeral. It was not all that impressive for one such as you."

"You think yours will be better than this? For someone as reclusive as you, I'd seriously doubt that."

Twenty minutes later we materialized inside Manaan's ship. Lugh and Angus sat at the table playing some kind of game. Lugh looked up when we appeared. "That was timely! I just finished beating Angus at this game of bones. How was the funeral?"

I went over and perched on his knee, giving him a hug. "Opulent!" I exaggerated. "It was packed and there were oceans and oceans of flowers."

Flidais took a seat across from Angus. "It was depressing. But the good news was we didn't see any strange men hanging around. They've probably given up, as they should."

Manaan walked into the room and smiled. "Are your friends going to be here soon? No change of plans in that, I hope. I have guards on shore waiting to escort them aboard."

I noticed Flidais roll her eyes before she spoke. "I thought they would wait until your parents were ready. Prudence is fine but Darby gets on my nerves. She's pretty full of herself considering that she's just a mortal." She looked over at Angus. "She's not at all powerful like me."

Seeing the flare of jealousy in her eyes, I held my tongue. And from the look in Angus's eyes, it was obvious even without reading his thoughts that he was still in love with Flidais. But I knew better than to interfere. The last time I'd done that, had been a disaster.

Still, I couldn't help myself when I blurted. "I'm letting my mom tell Seth the truth about all of this. Flidais suggested it at the funeral. She's anxious to get to know him and my parents." I smiled at my sister. "Seth is pretty good looking, even if he is my brother."

I didn't dare look directly at Angus for his reaction but I caught some of it out of the corner of my eye. He actually flinched when Flidais added.

"He's *handsome*, Bernadette! Why wouldn't I want to know him better?" She winked at me and I knew that she had picked up on what I was trying to do.

Angus stood up and strode across the small room. "I need some fresh air, Manaan. If you would be so kind as to open the hatch and lower the gangplank, I'll wait with your men for Darby and Pru."

Manaan looked over at me and then Flidais before he spoke. "Certainly. I need to know how many beds I need to make up tonight though. This craft is fluid and I can accommodate many guests but I'm a minimalist. I like to have just what is actually needed."

Angus's eyes narrowed when he glanced at Flidais. "I can probably bunk in with Darby. She didn't mind the first time that happened."

Oh shit. Our teasing had gone too far. Up to this point,

Angus had resisted Darby's advances, but now he was reverting to the old womanizing Angus-- even if it was payback for Flidais's remark about my brother.

I looked over at Flidais. She suddenly feigned an interest in the board game on the table, purposely ignoring Angus.

Lugh squeezed my knee and I knew he was thinking the exact same thing I was.

This was going to be a tense trip when we left. Things weren't getting any better between Angus and Flidais. And Darby's inclusion was adding fuel to the potential explosion between them.

And not only that, but there was the discussion that I needed to have with my parents. Darby and Prudence weren't the only ones who should be resettling in New Zealand. As long as there was anyone alive who knew about me, they would never be safe in the States.

Twenty Seven

Darby and Prudence arrived a few hours later with suitcases in hand. Prudence rushed over to hug me, and then took a seat next to me on the sofa. Her face was tight when she spoke.

"That was awful. Your funeral was hard but saying goodbye to my own family tore my heart out. I hope that someday I'll be able to return and be with them again."

Her words brought tears to my eyes. None of this would have happened if not for me. Before I got a chance to apologize, Darby chimed in.

"It won't be forever, Pru. This is a chance to start our lives in a virtual paradise. We'll own beachfront homes, do whatever job interests us or do nothing at all."

She looked over at me. "Your brother has changed a lot since we were kids, Bernadette. He's gone from being a total pain in the butt to being pretty nice. Even though he was heartbroken about you at the funeral and afterwards at your parent's home, he spent time making sure Pru and I were included in everything."

"Well, that's good to hear. I'm kind of glad that my folks are gonna tell him the truth. He might come along with us to New Zealand. I hope so." But even as I said it, I knew there was more that she wasn't saying. She was attracted to Seth! Things just got even weirder, considering that Flidais had also shown an interest in my brother.

Angus stepped over to Darby and put his hand on her cheek. Uh oh. I knew the power of a god's touch. After he'd made that remark about the sleeping arrangements, it was clear what he was up to. "I am looking forward to helping you set up your home in this far away place. You say it is a paradise but you have never seen Ethereal world. You will love it, Darby. It's a joyful place of love, song and dancing. "

Darby's eyes opened wider and she jerked away fast. "I'm not going to your world, Angus!" She kept edging away until she was backed up against the table. "Why would you think that's what I want?"

Angus blinked a few times looking at her. "You liked the time we spent together when we first met. That could be us again. You asked me to your new home, as well! We are both sensual, enjoying the finer things that life has to offer. Think of the babies—"

"No! Not going to happen, Angus." Darby's tones softened, "When you first came to our apartment in the Bronx, I thought you were human, like me. I admit I was still a little star struck when you showed up to help Bernadette, but anything between us can never happen again. You...you're kind of an alien, Angus. How old are you, anyway?"

Flidais snorted, "I doubt he's even a millennia old. Barely a child, no?" She smiled over at Angus. "What is it? Three or four hundred years?"

Darby's mouth dropped before she blurted, "What? I'm only twenty-three! Eew! You're not only a different species, you're *ancient!* Don't get me wrong. I like you and it was fun flirting a bit but what happened before between us is never going to happen again."

I didn't need to be a mind reader to see the hurt in Angus. He'd been rejected by my sister and now a mere mortal was casting some serious shade on his proclivity to be the renowned lover.

Lugh stood up and went over to Angus. I didn't hear what he murmured to his friend but whatever it was didn't cheer Angus up much. I couldn't help but wonder how much of Darby's rejection was due to the fact that she'd met my brother and had designs on him. Shallow, but that was Darby when it came to men.

Manaan tried to ease the tension in the room when he offered, "Have you eaten yet, ladies? I would be happy to provide whatever dishes you wish before you retire for the night."

Prudence answered for both of them. "We ate a ton of food at Bernadette's parents' place. That's what we do here, when a person dies. We eat and eat and eat. But thanks Manaan. You have been very kind to us."

Darby nodded. "Yes, Thank you, Manaan." Her cheeks flushed a deep pink and she added. "No offense about the alien thing, Manaan. I know you are a god as well. I didn't mean any disrespect."

The old man clapped her shoulder softly. "None taken. We are different species, but we can still be friends." He turned to Lugh. "Son, if it is all the same to you, I am going to take my leave and retire to my quarters. The last few days have taken more out of my old body than I would have expected."

There was a sly smile on his face when he added, "I trust you can sort out the sleeping arrangements."

I had to turn my face to hide the smile that twitched.

The crafty old god had left Lugh to deal with the hornet's nest of emotions.

Angus cleared his throat and then he added, "I will retire to my room as well. As for tomorrow, it is time for me to visit my homeland. It has been too long since I have danced with my people, enjoyed love and laughter." He looked over at me. "I'm sorry Bernadette, but I have grown weary of your world."

And with that he headed out of the state room to another part of the ship.

There was a sheepish look on Darby's face when she looked over at me. "I'm sorry if I spoke out of line and hurt his feelings. I'm too young to be tied down with anyone, let alone an *alien god*." Her eyebrows rose, "If I had to be with someone, it would be with someone here, maybe even Seth. Who knows?"

Flidais sneered at Darby. "You will never have a better offer than what that Fae Prince just proposed. You are not worth even a hair on that god's head." She stood up. "I have had enough of this day. I will see you in the morning."

Darby stuck her tongue out at Flidais when Flidais's back was turned leaving the room. She turned to me. "How can she really be your actual sister? She's a total bitch, Bernadette. I wish she'd go home with Angus. At least then this trip could be more fun."

Prudence snapped at her before I could respond. "Enough, Darby! You flirted with him and then when you met Seth, everything changed. You could have been a little less direct with him and still gotten the message across. Sometimes, diplomacy isn't your strong suit. I don't blame Flidais for calling you out."

"Sheesh! I'm only speaking the truth! Gods and mortals don't mix. Ask Bernadette! She started this whole thing back in Ireland with her stupid song. Since then everything's gone sideways."

Lugh's voice was deadly quiet when he spoke, "*Nothing*

Bernadette has done is wrong. Her song was *not* stupid. You are tired, Darby. I suggest you also retire to your room. I will show you the way."

"I'll keep you company, Darby." Pru got to her feet. She sighed and looked at me before she left. "This is going to be some trip, Bernadette. I'll see you in the morning."

I sat at the table thinking, hoping that my parents joining us would ease the tensions that had bubbled to the surface. Keeping the peace on board was gonna take some nimble footwork. After all that had happened, I wasn't sure that I was up for the task. But considering I'd attended my own funeral that day, I guess that was understandable.

Twenty Eight

I could hardly believe it was morning already when Manaan tapped on the door to our room. Lugh stretched and then pulled me into his arms. "Stay here for just another little while. I'd rather face an army of Fomorians than face any more drama between Darby and Flidais."

I snuggled in closer and kissed his neck. "It's only gonna get worse when Seth gets here. But at least Angus won't be here to be hurt again. I feel so bad for him. It's ironic. When I met him, he was always full of himself, ready to make babies with anyone and everyone. Now he's broken."

Lugh sighed. "He will survive. He needs some time with his people." When Faellin let out a whine and nudged Lugh with his nose, Lugh threw the coverlet back. "I'd better see to my dog, Bernadette. Nature is calling him."

174

"*My dog,* you mean! But sure, knock yourself out taking him for a walk." I yawned and then swung my legs over the side of the bed. I wasn't sure what time my parents and Seth would arrive but it was best to get up and ready for them. Plus, Darby and Prudence might feel awkward out there with only Manaan to keep them company at breakfast. Yet, that might be easier than if Flidais was also out there sniping at Darby.

Fifteen minutes later, freshly showered and dressed in a bright blue hoodie and jeans I was fixing my hair when again there was a tap at the door. I set the brush down and opened it. My jaw fell open seeing Flidais and Angus standing together, his arm around her waist. Even if I didn't read their thoughts, it was clear that they'd spent the night together.

"Hey! What's up?" I stepped back inviting them into the room. Angus practically sparkled as he followed my sister, who also kind of glowed.

Flidais looked shyly over at Angus and she seemed a bit tongue tied when she spoke. "Well...I went to console Angus last night after your friend--"

"You did a lot more than *console* me, Flidais! I've never spent such a night and that's saying something!" Angus pulled her close and planted a kiss on her forehead.

Flidais blushed and snuggled in closer, putting her arm around him as well. "I realized what I'd done to Angus, thanks to Darby's words. It wasn't much different than when I'd rejected Angus's offer of marriage in Otherworld. I was being shallow and selfish, setting aside the one who truly loved me."

"Adored you, is more accurate. I still do! But I'm not pressuring you into marriage. That will happen when and if you're ready. I'm happy to just be with my fair Flidais." Angus grinned from ear to ear, lifting her hand to kiss it.

I could hardly believe my eyes seeing them together and obviously so in love. My eyes welled with happy tears and I hugged the both of them. "So you're not going to Ethereal today? We can enjoy a vacation together? We've never had a moment where we can just *be*, enjoying ourselves without the threat of Fomorians, Aine or people here trying to abduct me."

Flidais actually giggled. "It will be a honeymoon without the trappings of marriage. I hope this New Zealand place is as beautiful as you say."

I eased back and felt the stress leave my shoulders. "I've never been there but photos look like the place is pretty much a Paradise."

"That's good enough for me! As long as I have my awesome goddess at my side, I will be ecstatic. I will even teach you to dance, Flidais. What sweet music we'll make together." Angus swung my sister in a circle and dipped her, before pulling her up and planting a kiss on her lips.

"I'm thrilled seeing the two of you together. And I promise, I will never interfere in your relationship again." I put my arms around them and added, "Now let's have something to eat!"

When we entered the main room a banquet was laid out on the enormous table. I looked around, wondering how Manaan did it. The ship really was fluid, able to accommodate whatever and whoever entered. Darby and Pru were already there just finishing up from stuffing themselves on every kind of fruit and pastry imaginable.

The gangway door opened and I smiled seeing Lugh and Faellin enter. He glanced at Flidais and Angus and then winked at me.

"Look who was wandering around outside when I took Faellin out." He stepped into the room and I saw my mother and father behind him.

"Bernadette!" My mother rushed over and hugged me, with my father not far behind. It was then that I noticed Seth enter, gaping at everything in the room with a look of disbelief.

His mouth opened and closed a couple of times before he managed to get the words out. "What kind of ship is this? I didn't even see it from outside and suddenly I'm inside this...whatever the heck you would call it."

I stepped over to him and gave him a hug. "It's a ship, Seth. Actually, it's close to being a submarine. Don't try to over think this, bro, cause it will drive you batshit crazy."

"Too late for that, I suppose." His eyes grew bigger, staring at me. "Mom and Dad filled me in but I still can't process all this. I'm at your funeral one day and here in some kind of magical ship with you the next. What the heck?"

"I'm sorry about all that, Seth. I guess you've heard the truth about me...you know being a Celestial goddess and all."

"Bernadette! This is crazy! And look what you put Mom and Dad through! Your *funeral?* You just about gave Dad a heart attack." He looked around at the other gods. "Who are these people? What kind of cult have you got mixed up in? That's not bad enough, but now you're dragging *us* into it too?"

I'd known it would be hard trying to explain all this to my brother but he was starting to get on my nerves. "It's not a cult, Seth!"

Mom came over and stepped between us. "I know this is difficult, Seth but we've seen Bernadette do some impossible things, right before our eyes. She can create things out of thin air. That's why everyone was after her. She had to do what she did...the funeral was part of her strategy."

Ignoring my mother's attempt to calm my brother, I darted to the side, glaring at him. "These are my friends and my biological sister, Seth. If not for them I would have died...*more than once!* You need to calm down and open your mind a bit. Not everything can be pigeonholed or categorized like you'd like, you know."

My father came over and put his arm over Seth's shoulders. "Sit down, son. Have a drink if that will help. All of this is true. Believe me, your mother and I experienced it. Your sister knows what she is doing. For once you'll have to have faith in her."

I noticed Darby shift over so that Seth could sit next to her. She took his hand, "Bernadette is setting us up in New Zealand. We will be wealthy, living like the rich and famous. You'll see, she's gonna fix this for you and your parents."

Even though Seth still didn't look convinced, it was becoming awkward with Lugh scowling at my brother. Angus stood with his arms crossed over his chest while Flidais glared...I could hardly look at my powder-keg sister. I took a deep breath and smiled. "Let me introduce my friends." I took Lugh's hand, "Mom, Dad, you've met Lugh and Angus and Flidais, but Seth, you haven't. They are gods—"

"I'm a Celestial!" Flidais interrupted. Her smile bordered on being a sneer as she stared at my brother. "Lugh is Tuatha de Danaan and this is Angus Mac Og, Fae Prince and my..." she looked at him with puppy dog eyes, "...my beloved."

I couldn't miss the triumphant look she shot at Darby. But Darby only had eyes for Seth. Okay, that was one battle that had been circumvented. Meanwhile, my mother and father gaped at the ship and the feast of food set out for them.

My mother looked over at Manaan, "You are a god like Bernadette? I owe you so much for all that you have done for my family. I understand that the Navy Seal team was actually your men that you sent to guard my husband and me."

Manaan approached my mother and lifted her hand, stroking her fingers. "My thanks is seeing you and Bernadette safe. Perhaps you will join me in a drink at the waterfalls in the moonlight this evening, to celebrate."

MORTAL ENEMIES (Celtic Knot #3)

I watched my mother's face flush like a schoolgirl's at the handsome old god's attention. For a moment she was actually tongue-tied: my mother, of all people! Even Dad noticed when he put his arm around Mom and pulled her close to him.

He smiled but there was an evenness in his voice when he commented to Manaan. "That would be lovely. My wife and I will enjoy that very much." His forehead tightened and he asked, "We can be all the way around the world by tonight? That's impossible. An airliner takes eighteen hours to get there."

Manaan grinned but he stepped back, letting go of my mother's hand. "We'll be there in time for dinner, Lanny. Just as soon as everyone is done with breakfast, I'll get this ship moving." He looked over at Angus. "Fae Prince? I take it you have changed your mind on leaving us?"

Angus beamed a smile at Flidais. "Someone else changed my mind. I'm looking forward to dancing on the beach with my Celestial queen."

My father stared at me from under his bushy eyebrows. "This is it, then? We will be living in New Zealand to avoid your enemies. Our lives, our home in Westchester where you were raised...that's all gone, now. This is a lot to take in, Bernadette. This place you set us up in better be a mansion, is all I can say."

Mom's head tipped as she looked up at him. "We never took many vacations, Lanny. It may not be forever and in the meantime, let's make the best of it. Bernadette won't let us down."

Seth peered at Flidais with narrow eyes. "You're actually Bernadette's blood sister? I mean you look like her but you're older, right?"

Instead of being insulted by my brother's comment, Flidais laughed. "I'm not *that* old! By your years, perhaps; but I'm quite young where I come from." Her eyes narrowed watching my parents and Seth. "You are a family.

I never experienced that when I grew up. Tell me what it's like."

Seth's eyebrows flew up, "That's hard to describe. I don't know where to start."

I tried to lighten the mood. "We've got a few hours, bro. But if you'd rather I told her my version of you tormenting me, painting mustaches on my Barbie dolls and putting glue in my nail polishes then I'd be happy to enlighten everyone."

Mom tsked, "Flidais, at times it seemed like Lanny and I were referees more than parents. But Bernadette was no picnic either. Remember the time you put chewing gum in the wheels of Seth's roller blades. I thought he'd murder you."

I sneaked a peek at Flidais who leaned closer, listening hard, even though she'd have no idea what a Barbie or roller blades even were. When Dad chimed in, her eyes lit up.

"We had to turn our faces many times so that you wouldn't see us laugh. Those were the days. And now, here we are in some fantastical dream with our children travelling at the speed of light to a tropical paradise." He looked over at Mom, "You packed my heart meds, didn't you?"

Angus stepped forward. "Lanny? I can help you with any health problems you have. It is one of my many gifts. I am a great healer."

"I don't think anyone can fix it." Seth snorted. "The best we can do is manage the symptoms with meds. Trust me, I've got years of medical training under my belt."

Angus smiled. "I'm sure you're very good at healing people here on earth, but I too am skilled, having trained under Devi, a powerful Druidess. Would you mind if I give it a try, Lanny?"

My father's eyes were big as saucers looking at Seth and then Angus. But it was my mother who broke the impasse.

"Why not let him try, Lanny? I did bring your meds but wouldn't it be wonderful if we could toss the pills overboard?" Her forehead knotted when she looked at Manaan, "Can I do that? Where is the railing and port windows?"

Seth threw his hands in the air. "Hey! I've stepped through the looking glass. As long as you don't do some kind of heart surgery on him, knock yourself out, Angus. But don't say I didn't warn you."

Angus stepped close to my father and placed his hands on the left side of Dad's chest. I could feel my throat tighten and it was hard to fight the tears that threatened to spill as I watched. I had seen Angus heal so many others (myself included when a guard had shot me with an arrow), that I knew this would work. Why hadn't I thought of this before?

In the meantime, Manaan snapped his fingers and the table was clear of food and used dishes. Lugh stepped close to me and held my hand, leaning down to whisper in my ear, "Your father will need a strong heart for this voyage. Remember how nauseous you were, the first time you rode in this ship?"

I smiled at him. "Oh yeah. Please don't be upset with my brother, Seth. He's trying his best to understand but this is totally out of left field for him."

"Field? I thought he trains to be a healer? He's also a farmer?" His eyes danced. "Your people's figures of speech are sometimes hard to follow, my dear."

I just shook my head at him.

Angus stepped back from my father and I peered closely to see the results. Dad's complexion which had always been a bit on the pasty side now showed a healthy shade with a tinge of pink in his cheeks. Even his eyes looked clearer.

"I feel lighter, somehow." Dad jumped to his feet and took a deep breath, clapping his hands to his chest. "Holy cow! I'm like I'm in my twenties again!" He stepped over to Flidais and took her hand, swinging her in a fox trot step dance as he hummed. "I thought I'd share my first dance as a new man with my newest eldest daughter!"

Then he moved on to me twirling me under his arm before lifting me up off my feet. "Bernadette! I can't tell you how wonderful it is to feel like this! I take back my words from earlier. Feeling like this is giving me a new lease on life."

"Lanny!" My mother was up and throwing herself into my father's arms. "Just take it easy. I know you feel better but…"

Angus looked over at Seth. "Your father is cured. He'll live many, many years more."

Darby threw her arms around Seth. "Isn't that great! I'm so happy for you." When Seth tried to disengage himself to join my parents, Darby hung on tight.

Manaan interrupted the laughter. "If you will take your seats in, we will disembark. If any of you feel squeamish, let me know and I'll make adjustments." He looked over at Prudence. "Would you like to join me in the control room? You might enjoy the sights, the currents and underwater life more, from a spot up front."

She grinned as she stood up. "Absolutely! I've scuba dived and even tried skin diving! I love the ocean! This will be amazing."

When she and Manaan left, I helped get my parents settled in, "This vessel is crazy fast, Mom. But fun! You're in for a wild ride."

At the sound of Flidais's voice singing that song that I'd sang at the Moon Pond and Angus joining in, playing the flute, I looked over at them. Perfect. If my family and friends were at all nervous about what was about to take place, the song would calm their nerves.

I snuggled in next to Lugh and he squeezed my hand. "Sing to me, Bernadette. This time it is only for pure pleasure, hearing your voice. I have missed that since you returned here. But now we're together once more."

So much had happened since that first time at the moon pond that it was hard getting the words out. A few times my voice cracked as I sank into his arms, gazing at my parents and brother sitting next to Darby. I had my family here, along with my sister, Angus and Lugh. Things weren't perfect, not with my brother still in a state of disbelief and even a little ticked off at what I'd done. But it was a start.

This was a time that I would look back on and miss—especially after New Zealand.

Twenty Nine

A few days later...

I stood in the living room of the bungalow which I'd convinced my parents to rent. It was way less ostentatious than the mansion which Mom had tried to wheedle for them. But for our purposes, it was perfect: a modest house, sitting across the road from a beautiful beach, in a relatively small coastal town on the South Island.

Dad had surprised me when he started looking at cars and boats and even a four wheeler. He'd been a lawyer all his life and now he suddenly wanted to live like Richard Branson, although without the plane, thank goodness. Much as I wanted my family to be comfortable, they were taking comfort to a whole new level. Nothing was too good or too expensive for them. I'd spent most of my time trying to reason with them that it wasn't good to attract too much attention.

Surprisingly, the only one who hadn't put too much pressure on me was my brother. But the reason was obvious when he and Darby entered the room, hand in hand, simpering over each other like lovebirds.

They flopped down on the leather sofa and Darby yawned before she spoke. "I overdid it with swimming and snorkeling today. I'm ready for a siesta."

Seth laughed. "Wrong country for that, Darb. But I'll keep you company." He looked over at me. "Are you joining us for dinner and then a campfire on the beach? We haven't seen that much of you since we got here, Bernadette. It'd be nice for all of us to get together tonight."

I smiled at him. He had no idea how hard I'd worked to make the arrangements for Mom and Dad as well as for him, Darby and Pru to live here. There were the passports, the arrangements with the bank, depositing money I'd conjured, not to mention securing the two homes I'd rented for them. Now, everything was set up and I could relax knowing that the chances of Bloomstein or those government agents finding any of them would be slim.

"It might be one of the last nights we all have a chance to be together for a while. I think Manaan is getting antsy about staying much longer. And Angus and Flidais are planning on visiting his homeland soon, so I *will* join you."

Darby's forehead knotted and she leaned forward, "Have you seen Pru today? She wasn't at the beach and she left before we got out of bed this morning."

"She went out in the vessel with Manaan. There's a reef about a mile out that she wanted to check out. Pru is definitely in her element here with all the marine life. I'm not sure she'll ever go back to the States to live." At the sound of footsteps and a playful bark, I looked over to see Lugh and Faellin enter the room from the wrap-around deck outside.

He walked over and planted a kiss on my cheek. "Are you ready to go for our walk to the waterfall? Faellin needs some exercise and I'd like some of his wine." He noticed Seth and Darby sitting there, "You want to join us?"

Darby shook her head. "We'll take a pass on the hike but save some wine. I never thought I'd like the wine that comes from that dog's coat but it's awesome. Bring some to dinner and to the bonfire on the beach, Lugh."

She rose and then tugged at Seth's hand, pulling him to his feet. "Let's go, babe. We've got the house to ourselves with Pru gone!"

I smiled seeing my brother's cheeks flush a bright pink. But he made no move to stop her when she giggled and raced towards the door. He did a finger wave and then the two of them were gone, racing across the yard towards the bungalow that they shared.

Lugh's eyebrows lifted high and he grinned. "It looks like Darby is wearing your brother out, not that he's complaining." His hand brushed my cheek and he gazed down at me. "Which brings me to the question of us. When are we returning to Otherworld? I've come to a decision about us ruling there, side by side. I quelled the rebellion which was fermenting but there will be more, until the kingdom is restored to its glory. We should return soon."

I felt a heaviness in my gut at his words. "There's always war and battles there, Lugh. What's the hurry? I thought you were enjoying our time here in New Zealand. At least we don't have to look over our shoulders waiting for your enemies or mine to attack us. It's nice to have a break from all that."

Lugh pulled back and blinked a few times staring at me. "But Bernadette, this is what you wanted. You left my world when I couldn't agree to have you rule beside me. Now I am offering it to you."

Sighing, I nodded. "I know. But I'm tired of always

fighting, trying to stay ahead of bad-ass thugs. I was kidnapped, Lugh, and then they *killed* me!"

Seeing the shock in his eyes, I added. "I'm grateful to you, that you came and saved me, don't get me wrong. But my life feels like I'm out of control, with everyone wanting a piece of me. My mom and dad barely agreed to not living in a mansion. Darby and Pru expected maid service and unlimited bank accounts, not to mention new vehicles including yachts and Seadoos. I've been busy looking after everyone, Lugh!"

Lugh's eyes became flinty. "This is the burden and responsibility of being a god, Bernadette. You must protect your family and friends from enemies which you made. There are bad things in my world as well as in yours. We don't give up because we are *tired*. Evil doesn't give up and neither can we."

I sank down onto a large boulder at the end of the driveway. Suddenly, the thought of hiking to the waterfall, no matter how beautiful it was, drained my last ounce of energy. I looked up at him. "My life used to be simple, Lugh. My only worry was making sure I got enough shifts at the restaurant to pay my share of the rent. Since I met you, it's been a rollercoaster of danger. I actually *died*, Lugh!"

But if I expected him to understand his next words shattered that hope.

His face clouded. "I am disappointed in you, Bernadette. When we met, you were feisty and even fierce. And that was when we didn't know of your lineage. Now that you have come into your own, a *Celestial*, you shy away from your responsibility? That is not the woman I fell in love with."

If he'd called me lazy and worthless he could not have hurt me more than when he'd said he was disappointed in me. "That's not fair, Lugh. You've known your status all your life. You were raised to be a god, ruling your kingdom. I've only known of my power for a very short time. It's a *lot* to take in. I need time and just a little space from it for a while."

Lugh shook his head slowly. "You don't have that luxury, Bernadette. I need you at my side. Your parents and your friends need you to provide a safe shelter." He rolled his eyes, "Which would not have been necessary if you'd stayed with me in Otherworld. You brought danger to their doorsteps with your rash behavior. They will always need your help because of this, unless you bring them with you to Otherworld."

Oh god. He was totally not getting it. Not by a long shot. He was actually adding pressure at a time when what I really needed was his understanding. "That will never happen, Lugh. It's bad enough that they had to move half-way around the world but to introduce them to *your* world? Even *I'm* not ready to step back into the chaos there, with enemies always lurking. I just need to step back from all this for a bit."

"You're an entitled coward, Bernadette."

That was it. I stood up and practically spat my next words, "A coward? I don't think so! Since I met you," I used my fingers to count off each point, "I've been chased, attacked and kidnapped by Fomorians, held Tully the Banshee as she lay in my arms dying, was manipulated by my treacherous mother, Aine, fought alongside my sister to kill that woman, came back home only to find the mafia, a psycho billionaire and the government after my powers."

My teeth ground together at the next point, "And then I *got killed* and attended my own funeral and had to flee with all of you to save my family and friends. Even my parents and friends keep asking for more from me...bigger houses, cars, boats, a lifestyle for the rich and famous!"

I'd run out of fingers so I put my hands on my hips for the next point. "So yes, I think I need a break from being a goddess. Things were way more simple when I slung drinks for a living."

Lugh was silent for a few moments, just staring at me

with anger. His face changed, like a mask had fallen over it, vaporizing every emotion. "I can see that your mind is made up. Enjoy your life here, Bernadette. I will be returning to Otherworld to rule my kingdom, as a god should."

He whistled at Faellin who had wandered off a bit. When the dog returned he held its collar and took off heading for the trail to visit the waterfall.

I sat there for a long while watching him leave until he was out of sight, hidden in the thick trees. Tears rolled down my cheeks and I did nothing to stop them. I had no energy to argue with Lugh or listen to my parents gripe about their new life. I just had nothing left to give anyone right then.

When Angus and Flidais showed up I had no idea how long I'd been sitting there. Flidais knelt down in front of me and took my hands in hers.

"What's wrong Bernadette? Is it Lugh? Has he said or done something to upset you?" She tucked a stray lock of hair behind my ear. "Tell me."

Seeing the concern in her eyes, my tears began again. "I told him I'm not going back to Otherworld to rule with him. He's upset. He's leaving soon."

"But why? I want you to come with us. Your parents are fine. Darby and Seth are happy and Prudence has found her life's calling, studying marine life."

I shook my head. "But that's just it! Everyone is fine but *I'm* not. I don't know why but everything is hitting me all at once. Stepping back into a life of death and destruction is too much right now. That's what a life with Lugh would be like—fighting and enemies and…"

"But that's *life*, Bernadette! You're tired. But things will get better." When I didn't respond she turned to Angus. "Fix her! Use whatever healing you have to restore her energy."

Angus shook his head. "I wish I could, believe me. But Bernadette's illness is in her will. I fix bodies but the mind is another thing altogether." He touched my cheek and sighed.

"What you need is rest."

Flidais gave my shoulder a shake. "Stay with me at my home. I will care for you and bring you back to yourself. We will run in the forest and have fun."

Even that didn't perk me up. "No, but thanks. I think I need a break from being a Celestial. I want to return to a simpler life. No enemies kidnapping me. My family and friends are also sucking the life out of me." Seeing the hurt in her eyes, I added. "Not you or Angus, Flidais. It's my parents and Darby. They keep asking for more and more...stuff."

Angus sighed. "I've seen this happen to some men who have been in battle. They function fine while fighting but afterwards, the horror of it all cripples them. Take time for yourself, Bernadette. You've done all you could for your family and friends. Now you need to take care of Bernadette."

I looked up at him through teary eyes. He was telling me what I'd already realized in my gut. I needed to be on my own for a while. Instead of taking care of everyone around me, I needed to simplify my life.

Until I could do this, I had nothing left for Lugh or anyone else.

Thirty

Two months later...

I glanced at the clock hanging over the oak bar as I swiped a damp cloth over the table. It was almost nine in the evening, the end of my shift at Kirby's, a local watering hole in Tralee, Ireland. I pocketed the few Euros, left by the rugby players who were in town finishing a tournament, celebrating their win with copious pints of Guinness.

"Would you care for a drink with me, lass, before you clear out? Take a load off your feet and have a few laughs?" Colin Devonshire leaned over the table where he sat alone, nursing his beer.

My reply was the same as it had been every night since I'd been working there. "Thanks, Colin, but I've left my dog on his own for too long. The poor bugger will be bustin' a gut to get out for a walk." Thankfully, Lugh had left Faellin with me before he'd gone back to Otherworld. Not only was Faellin good company, he provided an excuse to avoid not only Colin's offer but a few others as well.

"Another time, then? Can you bring me another before you take off, darlin'?" It was the same response he always came back with.

Sometimes it felt like I'd stepped onto the set of 'Groundhog Day'. Despite the monotony, it was peaceful. I poured another draft for Colin and then wandered over to where he sat in the corner of the dimly lit bar. "Here you go. I put it on your tab."

"You're a saint, Saint Bernadette." He chuckled, even though he'd made the same joke every night.

I rolled my eyes and smiled. Colin was good looking in a rustic kind of way, even though he was way too old for me, in his early forties. But as the other waitresses had told me, it was no wonder his wife had left him. She couldn't compete with the bar for his attention.

After hanging up my apron, I signaled to Gus who was manning the bar, although most of his time was spent watching the sports match on the TV. "G'night, Gus! See you tomorrow!" He waved his hand but his head never turned from the game.

Outside, the cool damp air seeped under the collar of my wool jacket as I walked home. It was funny. Winter at home in New York had been brutal with the tall buildings creating wind funnels that would freeze you solid. Here, the temperature never dipped down to that freezing point but the dampness went right through you. Walking along the waterfront with the grey waves rolling in to shore, made it seem even more bleak, despite the brightly colored shops I passed by.

MORTAL ENEMIES (Celtic Knot #3)

An elderly couple walking towards me caught my eye. The woman with her bleached hair under the knit tam made me think of my mother. She and Dad were still in New Zealand living at the house I'd rented, beside Darby and Seth. Pru had moved to Christchurch to begin studies at the university there. We Skyped a few times a month, now that they were over their anger at me for leaving so abruptly.

When I reached the townhouse that I'd rented, I could hear Faellin yip and scratch at the door as I unlocked it. "It's okay. I'm home, buddy." I barely had the door open before he nuzzled my hand, thumping his tail against my thigh. I grabbed the lead and snapped it onto his collar. "Just a short walk tonight, Faellin. It's going to rain any minute."

We walked down the block to the park which Faellin liked. Being so close to the ocean, I couldn't help but think of New York and the park in Queen's that he favored. That was a lifetime ago, when I'd loved the idea of being a goddess, a Celestial no less. Since moving to the town in Ireland, I'd purposely shed everything to do with that. It didn't mean I didn't miss Lugh and Angus and Flidais. But their lives were on Otherworld and mine was here...at least for now.

I passed by a fountain in the center of the park, heading for a copse of trees which Faellin considered his personal toilet. Anything to hurry this up to get home and have a hot bath. Darkness and the loneliness of the park weren't helping.

"Bernadette?"

I practically jumped out of my skin hearing the woman's voice. Turning around, my jaw fell open seeing Devi standing there. Even though she wore a wool overcoat and hat, there was no mistaking the ice blue eyes or the perfection of her face.

"Devi? What are..." My heart skipped a beat. "Oh no! Has anything happened to Lugh? Is he all right? Why are you here?" I rushed over to her side.

She clasped my hands in hers and sighed. "He's fine...or at least I hope he is. We haven't seen Lugh for over a fortnight. He was distraught when he came back to his kingdom, hardly leaving his quarters. But then one night he left. No one has heard a word about him."

My head pulled back in surprise as she talked. "Even you can't divine where he went? Is it the Fomarians? Did they kidnap him?" My heart leapt in my throat picturing Lugh at the hands of enemies like Morc and those horrid brothers."

She shook her head and her voice became softer. "Do you not think that I tried every tool at my disposal, Bernadette? No. He's gone. Somehow he has cloaked any trace of himself...or someone more powerful that I has done this to him."

I peered at her and without even trying, I picked up on the rest of her thoughts. "But that isn't the only reason you're here. It's Flidais." Again my mouth fell open, gaping at her. "She's pregnant? Oh my God!"

She shook her head, answering the question that had sprung to the surface in my mind. "No, she didn't do this by herself, like Aine did giving birth to you and Flidais. Angus is the father, even though he's not convinced of it. They quarreled and now she's back in her forest retreat. I tried to console and care for her, but she's turned into..." She gave her head an exasperated shake before continuing, "Let's just say that she's even more irritable and irritating than I'd ever thought possible."

I knew what she wanted; for me to return to Otherworld and help find Lugh and deal with Flidais. But I wasn't sure how I could help. If Devi couldn't locate Lugh, what chance would I have? As for Flidais, it sounded like hormones were driving her crazy. That would sort itself out in time. Angus would see when the child was born that it was his.

Devi wasn't giving up though. "You must help us find Lugh, Bernadette. With him gone, it won't be long before the Fomarians learn of the vulnerability of the kingdom. I had always thought that the kingdom would always be the most important thing in Lugh's life. It was until he met you, Bernadette."

I thought of the time when I'd first met Lugh, how he'd been banished in a spell from his kingdom. Even though he'd stayed by my side trying to fulfill a blood debt to me, it had been his dream to return and rule once more. Now that dream was broken and it was my fault.

Faellin came over, sniffing at Devi until I pulled him close to my side. It was a good distraction as I pondered Devi's words. But I knew Devi's ability well enough to hide my thoughts behind a metal fortress in my mind.

Devi's hands rose to give my shoulders a shake. "You must help Lugh and your sister! Even Angus is suffering because of the situation in Otherworld. Your place is there, not hiding here serving watered down ale to drunks."

I couldn't argue with her about that. Living a simple life in Tralee had served its purpose. I'd stepped away from my lineage but even as I'd done that, I'd always known it was a respite, not my life's goal. Faellin looked up at me with his sweet brown eyes, his emotions practically pouring out, agreeing with Devi. He let out a 'yap' and stood up, thumping his tail against my thigh.

"You want to find Lugh too, don't you boy? He was yours before you claimed me."

"Yap!"

I looked over at Devi.

"Let's go! I need to find Lugh and help my sister."

The END

Author's Note:

I truly hope you're enjoying this series! Writing it has been one of my most enjoyable times as an author. If you could leave a review for this book, I'd be very grateful.

I took a break from this series during the pandemic. I think it's my body's way of telling me that I need to return to Ireland to nourish my creative soul for this storyline. I tried three times to write book 4, but it wasn't working. So for now, this tale is done.

But I do intend to go back to this in the future.

Best Wishes to you and yours, dear reader.

Shelley Dorey

ABOUT THE AUTHOR

Michelle Dorey, writing as 'Shelley Dorey' is the author of more than a dozen spine-chilling novels featuring ghosts, haunted houses and the supernatural. She has been on the Amazon best seller list many times throughout her career.

A voracious reader of the masters like Stephen King and Dean Koontz, she decided to try her hand at writing after going on a Ghost Walk in the enigmatic city of Kingston, Ontario, Canada where she lives. Her first book, Crawley House was inspired by a true tale of a family's nightmare, living in a home owned by Queen's University.

"Expect the supernatural when the bedrock of a city is limestone. Throw in the fact it is bordered on three sides by the mighty St. Lawrence River, The Rideau River and Lake Ontario and you are in for some thrills and chills of the paranormal variety--which of course is my cup of tea."

Does she love Kingston? You bet! Her husband Jim, a transplanted native New Yorker born and raised in the Bronx, agrees. Michelle and Jim like nothing better than spoiling their two pugs with treats and long walks in their neighborhood. Funny, but the slightly neurotic dogs always refuse to go for a stroll in the cemetery nearby.

OTHER WORKS

All of Michelle Dorey and Shelley Dorey books are exclusively available on Amazon

Women's Paranormal Fantasy By Shelley Dorey

The Mystical Veil Series
Hex After 40 Series
Celtic Knot Series

Ghosts And Hauntings By Michelle Dorey

The Hauntings Of Kingston Series
The Haunted Ones Series
The Haunted Cabin